FITTING IN

THIS BOOK BELONGS TO:

FITTING IN

by

Sharon Kirsh

SECOND STORY Press

Thanks to Rhea Tregebov — clever and supportive guide.
— S.K.

CANADIAN CATALOGUING IN PUBLICATION DATA

Kirsh, Sharon L. (Sharon Louise), 1950–
Fitting in

ISBN 0-929005-74-0

I. Title.

PS8571.I67F58 1995   jC813'.54   C95-932108-X
PZ7.K57Fi 1995

Edited by Rhea Tregebov
Cover illustration by Kasia Charko

Second Story Press gratefully acknowledges the assistance of
the Ontario Arts Council and The Canada Council

Printed and bound in Canada

Published by

SECOND STORY PRESS
720 Bathurst Street, Suite 301
Toronto Canada
M5S 2R4

To the people I love,
there and here, then and now.
And especially to Mom, Malka, and Dan.

1

PHYLLIS AND I are inspecting ourselves in the small mirror hanging above the bathroom sink at Hebrew school. It is recess. With our stomachs pressed very close to the sink, our heads rubbing up cheek to cheek, both our faces can be squished into one glance. Phyl has to hunch over a bit to make it work because she's much taller than I am.

A sharp wind pitches autumn leaves against the window. Inside we're snug, inside where glossy pink tiles surround us. Everything — even the liquid soap that plops out of the dispenser — is bright pink.

"You're so lucky," Phyl says.

"Lucky? Me? Why?" I ask.

"Because you don't look very Jewish."

"What do you mean?" I lean in towards the mirror, blotting out Phyl's face.

"You know exactly what I mean. Look at my *nose*! It's big and ugly!"

She cocks her head to the left and stares at her reflection, a tiny smile on her lips. She does love herself a little.

"Looks fine to me."

"No, it doesn't!! When I'm older I'm going to have this shnoz fixed. At least I'll *look* more like the kids at public school. I stick out enough in other ways, why should I have to look weird too."

"Who says big noses are ugly? Who says Jewish noses are big?" I'm starting to take this as a personal insult. "Don't you like the way you are?"

"No! I don't. I want to fit in, not stick out. Like my stupid nose." She presses her hair away from her forehead. It forms a jagged black halo around her head.

"And look at my hair. It's frizzy. Yours is curly, but mine is black and frizzy. Not straight and shiny and blond. And this *nose* — it practically covers my *entire* face. Can't you *see*?"

Phyl and I have known each other since we were knee-high to a grasshopper. She's like a sister without the headaches. Why would I think she was ugly?

"Are you *dense*, Mollie? Think about the popular girls in our class at public school. They're so small and dainty and ... and smooth."

For the first time since birth, I am speechless.

"That's how I want to be, small and smooth. And that's exactly why I'm going to fix my nose. Mom says I can straighten my hair with that straightener, or I can go to the hairdresser to have it done if I want."

Phyl is one of the smartest people I know, so I can't dismiss her as a fool. She's probably right. All these years people have passed me in the street and thought to themselves, "Oh dear, what a frightfully ugly child. She must be Jewish. Poor thing."

My father picks me up after Hebrew school (we call it Hebe). It's a few minutes past six o'clock, dark enough to see my reflection in the car window as we pass under the street lights.

"What are you staring at?" he asks.

"Nothing."

What about my father? I redirect my attention to *his* nose. It's big, but is it Jewish? This requires more study.

When we arrive home, my mother, with her sweet face, is standing at the stove. My little brother Ray, adorable Ray, is racing his cars along the linoleum, and my handsome older brother Norman is solving math problems. I cannot believe that they need *their* faces fixed. I take off my coat and settle in.

During dinner I see nothing but nostrils and bridges. I am rivetted by the variety of nose shapes and lengths and movements situated around one kitchen table. Every breath in, every breath out, every nose twitch, every nose itch takes on a meaning it never had before.

After dessert, I dash from the table and find myself standing in front of the medicine cabinet mirror. The bathroom is softened by the fragrance of baby powder. I pick up the hand mirror with the pearly pink handle and, with my back to the sink, raise the hand mirror so that it's as high as my face but just off to the left. I raise it higher and higher, and tilt it until I can see the entire bushy back of my head. It's a mass of brown curls. It doesn't move when my head moves, it doesn't sway in the breeze. It is thick, a solid mass, serious.

Slowly, I pivot until the mirrors are positioned for side viewing. Time for the profile test. My hand is shaking, the mirror is shaking. I don't know what to expect. How bad can it be?

It's bad. Really bad. This is no cute little profile. This is a Nose. Phyl has known all along. I have lived in a fool's paradise.

Mid-discovery and the door rattles.

"Who's there?"

"It's your mother. Naomi is on the phone."

I love Phyl, but Naomi is my best friend.

In a flash I'm in the hallway, parked on the bench of our telephone table. My father has covered the seat cushion in plastic because I spend so much time sitting there he's afraid I'll wear it out. The wooden writing surface has a few gouges and nicks, long ago forgiven. We keep a small writing pad and a pen beside the telephone. I like to doodle while I talk, mostly flowers with long stems and women's eyes with long lashes.

"Mollie? Can we go over our math homework together?"

"Yup. Uh, before we do, can I ask you a question, Nao?" Sometimes I call her Nao (pronounced Nay-o) rather than Naomi because that extra syllable seems to jam itself in the way of the closeness between us.

"Sure." Naomi always sounds like the Voice of Doom. When she gets excited or upset, her eyelashes flutter in double time.

"Well, do you know what it means to 'look Jewish'?"

"Yes. I think I've known all my life."

"Really?? Why haven't I known it all *my* life?"

"Mollie, you're asking me these questions like I'm some kind of expert. All I know is what my mother told me. Lots of people hate Jews and always have."

"But why?"

"Because we're different. People think we're strange."

"Strange is the same as ugly?"

"I wish you'd take your questions to your mother! It's getting late and if you're not going to go over math with me, then I'll have to ask Moe to help me."

"Why would you ask your brother to help?!"

"Because the one thing he's good at is math."

"I guess everybody's got to have *one* talent." We both chuckle. We share a lot of chuckles over mopey Moe.

We review our math and then I run the bath water. This time I avoid my reflection.

want to stand up straight.

With the oath completed, we move along to the blood-letting ceremony. It is our first time. To be real blood sisters, each has to prick her own finger with a pin and then smear the shiny red droplet against the droplet on her blood sister's finger. This seals our sense of oneness.

We sit cross-legged on the round purple mat in the middle of my bedroom floor. The sewing needle rests on a pure white tissue on top of the mat.

"I think I'm going to faint," I whisper, hoping to call a temporary halt to the ceremony. Friendship aside, the whole business suddenly seems to have lost its logic.

"Take your time, Mollie. I'll go first."

Naomi steadies herself, inhales deeply and on the exhale pierces the skin of her fingertip. She grimaces. She sits waiting for my turn, supporting her upturned left pointer finger between the thumb and pointer of her right hand. Her droplet is turning into a thin red snake slithering towards her palm.

"Hurry up. Or I'll bleed to death."

There is no going back. Sickened, I lift the needle, tap it against my right pointer (I'm left-handed), and moan at the sight of a white fingertip.

Surgery has not been successful.

"It must be horrid being a pin cushion. Do it for me?"

"Really? Are you sure? What if I hurt you?" Naomi is uneasy at the thought of driving a metal spike, even a tiny one, through my finger.

She propels herself over to my side of the mat, grabs my right arm and sticks it under her left arm pit until it extends in front of her as though she has grown a third arm. Her black eyelashes flutter with anticipation. (I've always wondered whether her eyelids are unusually weary at night, but there is a limit to just how personal a question can be, even with your best friend.)

"I can't do it." She pushes away my arm.

"Thanks anyway, Nao. Here's a tissue for your finger."

For a moment she concentrates on rubbing her own blood from her hand, and then she looks straight at me and smiles. "I guess that shows how close we really are. We're blood sisters without even needing to share blood."

That's our kind of friendship ... we don't even need to share blood.

3

I WAKE UP to the pounding of heavy autumn rain-drops on my window. The curtains are sucked against the screen where the window is open. Time to get up, but the sun refuses to show its face. My room smells earthy and fresh.

Last night's telephone conversation with Naomi about "Jewish looks" is making its way back into my thoughts. I touch my nose. It feels swollen. Then I stroke, or perhaps I should say "bump along," my hair. After several minutes of considering what I'll have to face in the bathroom mirror, I drag myself out of my cosy linen cave.

The bathroom is cool and dim. It's better with the lights out, I think to myself as I wash up for school. In bright light there can be no secrets.

Naomi and Phyl are nowhere to be seen, but Elizabeth Anne is waiting for me outside school.

Elizabeth Anne wants to discuss math homework. I want to discuss noses.

"Elizabeth Anne," I position myself so that my profile is directly in front of her, "do you think I look Jewish?"

Her eyebrows crease. "No, not really. Well, sort of. Why?"

"I can't believe it!"

"Believe what?"

"I can't believe you understood the question. You *know*. You already know about 'looking Jewish,' don't you?"

"Sure. Who doesn't? Why do you want to know whether you look Jewish?"

Elizabeth Anne is my link to the Christian world. She is church-going and God-fearing, but more than that, in her home she has been taught tolerance. If *she* knows about looking Jewish (and even has a private opinion about my looks, which is the most aggravating aspect), then probably most people I know have been in on this for a long time.

"How long have you known about this 'looking Jewish' business? And what exactly do you mean? Which parts of my face are Jewish? And the other parts — are they some other religion? Like my ears, are they Moslem? And are my teeth Buddhist?"

By the final question, my voice is shrill. Elizabeth Anne seems annoyed.

"What's the big deal?" For Elizabeth Anne this is quite bold. "If you're so interested in this topic why don't you talk to your parents about it?"

"Fine!" I snort. "I thought we were friends. Now you won't even tell me what you think of me!"

Her hand flies to her cheek as though she has been slapped.

"Sorry," I mumble, out of obligation.

"It's okay," she mumbles back.

"I guess I don't like being the last to know a secret."

Elizabeth Anne shrugs and walks away.

4

I LOVE FRIDAYS. On Fridays, everybody seems lulled by daydreams of the weekend. I decide to put away this week's "Jewish looks" problem. After school Naomi and I go on one of our regular end-of-week expeditions to the shopping plaza near my house. These visits have nothing to do with shopping. They're just our way of letting our hair down at the end of the school week in a place where we won't be under anyone's watchful eye.

My father has told me about store detectives. They stroll about dressed in ordinary clothes spying on customers to make sure they don't shoplift. So in a sense we *are* under someone's watchful eye, but we're never certain who he is. Sometimes we guess that it's the man in the grey fedora, and then we follow *him* around the store until we come up with something more exciting to do, or until he gives us the "get lost" look.

When the last school bell rings on Friday afternoon, Naomi and I are always the first ones out the door, the first ones at the bus stop, and completely winded by the time we tumble through my front door.

My mother is standing in front of the kitchen sink plucking pinfeathers from the scrawny white chicken that will end up on our dinner plates.

"Mom, we're going to the shopping plaza for awhile, okay?"

"Okay. When will you be home?"

"Soon. Really soon."

My face flushes. Sometimes I want my mother to save me from myself. Sometimes I feel like I'm really two people: there's me and then there's my evil twin.

"Don't forget to be back within the hour. Would you girls like a snack before you go?"

Naomi is about to accept her offer, but I'm anxious to carry out our plan.

"No thanks, Mom. We're not hungry."

It's an outright lie. Naomi is always hungry, but she's too proper to contradict me in front of my mother. We drop our book bags and dart out the back door.

Even though the plaza is only two blocks away from my house, whenever we go there it's so dark and understated, so adult, that it feels like we're discovering a distant lost planet.

We whiz past the shoe store's dowdy display of sensible brown oxfords. In autumn and winter we rarely bother to window shop. You can tell that spring is coming when the dreary oxfords make way for gleaming white saddle shoes. Every year there's the same decision: whether to buy the ones with blue trim or the ones with brown trim. They're almost blinding in their whiteness. The very first time you walk out into the April sun there is a genuine "spring" in your step. The real nuisance about them is polishing the white leather that gets scuffed just by looking at it. I find that if I let mine get dirty enough, it's my mother who ends up using the elbow grease.

Up to the second floor of the plaza we trudge. All the shopping action is on the ground level. It's silent on the mezzanine, just a few offices scattered here and there. There's a black metal railing that overlooks the shoppers buzzing about below.

"Should we do it here, like we did last month?

Or should we go over there?" I want Naomi in on the planning.

"It doesn't matter. It works okay from any angle, really."

"Good. Let's go downstairs and buy what we need. Then we'll come back up."

The aroma of roasting salted nuts tempts us.

"A dollar's worth of pink pistachios, please."

Don't ask me why, but it's Naomi who always does the asking when we shop, even though she's normally much more shy with strangers than I am. It's a tradition. And we split the cost. It's a huge financial sacrifice, but there's no other choice. After experimenting on and off for the past two years with every shelled nut on the market, we've agreed that the pistachio is the best nut for the job.

In a flash we are up the stairs again, positioned against the railing. We have a bird's-eye view of the shoppers, a perfect panorama filled with balding heads, shaggy woollen caps slouching to one side, hairdos that look much more stylish from the front than from the top.

Naomi clutches the bag of nuts. "Let's crack them all first, okay?"

"Sure. And then we can take turns throwing."
We squat on the floor.

The system works like this: we crack open each nut using our front teeth as mini-can-openers. After removing the pulp, we eat it. The shells are laid to rest on our woollen mittens which are stretched to their maximum on the floor. It's a fail-proof system.

Our fingers take on the intense pink dye from the shells. Our lips tingle with the mixture of salt, dye and fear.

"You first," Naomi says solemnly. Playing is hard work for her.

"Sure." Naomi always insists that I take the first risk. "But you stay on the lookout. I want to start with a baldy. And then you can do *your* favourite."

She whispers, "The coast is clear."

A brief moment passes before my target strolls into sight. Then, as if washed ashore, he appears, unsuspecting. I raise my hand, lean over the railing, and with all the strength my pitching arm can muster, I let it fly.

"You beaned him! You beaned him!"

Together we crouch by the railing and peer

through the slats. The victim is rubbing his scalp, looking heavenward for an answer.

"You're getting really good at this," Naomi compliments me.

"Not bad, but not nearly as good as you."

We don't think of ourselves as the sorts who'd do anything hurtful, but we do enjoy beaning bald men.

On the way home, we debate the merits and demerits of the shopping plaza. It's the only plaza in our part of town, so there's not much choice, although we have considered branching out to the public library.

5

OUR PUBLIC SCHOOL is a long trek from home. We don't have to walk three miles through raging snowstorms (like our parents claim to have done), but it is a bus ride away. Truth is, my father drives me there every day on his way to work. Those of us who live more than walking distance are allowed to remain in school during lunch time. Everyone else goes home. We six "foreigners" go on the honour system. There's no teacher supervising us directly, although there are staff members who are supposed to keep an eye peeled. Fortunately they've got better things to do. We bring our lunches in paper bags, our drinks in thermoses, and we sit at our desks to eat. Naomi, Elizabeth Anne, Phyl and I are the girls; Kevin and Jeff are the others. Phyl eats lunch with us even though she's in another class.

Lunch hour is actually one and a half hours. It would be awkward to call it "lunch-one-and-a-half-hours," so it has been streamlined. We have a sense of belonging to a special club, all of us, that is, except for Jeff, whose taste in friends runs more towards the mature, so none of us qualifies. We include him only when, out of sheer boredom, he shows signs of interest.

Phyl opens Monday's luncheon festivities with a few jokes. Naomi gets into the spirit and finds herself chuckling. We always get just a bit excited when Naomi gets giggling. She has a sensitive plumbing system. If something tickles her funny bone, she'll usually end up darting to the bathroom. We never do know whether she makes it in time; she's too dignified to report.

"By the way, Naomi," Phyl interrupts herself, "How come you always wear skirts with elasticized waistbands?"

"Because the waists never fit exactly right, so my mom replaces them with elastic." She stands up to shake the crumbs from her plump, jiggly lap.

"Let's see that elastic." Phyl reaches out and grabs at the waistband on Naomi's grey flannel skirt. Like a dog straining to free itself from its master's hold, Naomi wrenches herself free, but not before Phyl manages to haul that skirt and white half-slip right down to Naomi's knees. And there she stands, her rounded belly stretching her undies and garter belt to their expandable limits.

It can go either way with Naomi. She is equally capable of roaring with berserkness as with laughter. Her laughter is contagious, but her berserkness is scary.

Slowly and deliberately she examines the space between her waist and her knees. Then her eyes fall to the floor, to the pool of grey flannel and white cotton lapping her ankles. A thin grin sprouts on her face. That grin widens until her lips burst open and an enormous guffaw, not just a titter, flies out. Immediately we join in, even Jeff.

And then we sense a change of atmospheric conditions. Naomi stands before us with her thighs squeezed together tightly, but it's too late. A puddle, just a tiny yellow puddle, drizzles onto the floor near her feet. It begins to flow down the aisle towards the teacher's desk. Jeff runs from the room disgusted. Kevin, out of respect for Naomi, leaves.

With the boys gone, Phyl, Elizabeth Anne and I gather around Naomi. We're prepared to be solemn. She gazes in disbelief at that glistening stream, and then presses her fingertips to her open lips. The grin tells us which way the wind is blowing.

"Get some paper towels from the washroom," she directs us. Phyl, Elizabeth Anne and I race out of the room, giddy with the embarrassment of it all.

"If Naomi tells on me, I'll be shot at sunrise," says Phyl in a half-worried, half-excited voice. Elizabeth Anne and I can only agree.

When we get back, we find Naomi dressed again in her skirt. It's sopping wet and smells like a bus terminal. She has rolled her half-slip into a small wet ball and has stuffed it into the paper bag that had held her sandwich and celery sticks. The paper is already turning mahogany brown in the wettest parts.

"Let's ask Mrs. Thorn in Home Ec to iron your skirt. That will dry it a bit." Phyl is feeling sheepish.

"Okay, but you do the talking if she's there."

She's there.

"What are you girls doing here during your lunch hour? You're really not supposed to be in here now."

"Sorry, Mrs. Thorn. Uh, Naomi spilled apple juice on her skirt while she was eating and she wondered whether we could iron it before the afternoon bell?"

"Take off your skirt, Naomi, and I'll do it. I don't want you girls using the iron."

We stand at attention beside Mrs. Thorn watching her prepare the iron. When it's warmed, she tests it on her ironing board. Next she flings Naomi's skirt over the pointy end of the board and positions it for blast-off. For two minutes she presses that garment with the skill her many years have earned her, and then she sniffs and turns from the board, iron in hand.

"Apple juice??"

We blush.

6

OUR CITY IS LARGE enough to call itself a "city,"
but it feels more like what you think of when
you hear the word "town." That's partly because
everybody seems to know everybody else's business. This is both good and bad. The good part is
that you always feel taken care of in bad times, and
the bad part is that in good times you feel like
you're in a fish bowl. On balance, it's a fine place
to be, especially since the ocean crashes against
the shore just on the outskirts of town, and the
crabby cawing of seagulls on the main streets
brings with it the salty mists. Harbour ferries blast
their foghorns. People walk slowly, not pushing to
get there — wherever "there" is. People talk slowly because there's time to listen.

Once in a long while a dreadful event occurs to
shake us from our trance. Two Julys ago, for

instance, a fifteen year old boy out for a bike ride after dinner shot and killed a seven year old girl. She was on her way out of a corner store, holding a cherry Popsicle in her hand. The boy had stolen his father's hunting rifle. It turns out he was what the people on the radio kept calling "emotionally disturbed." For a few weeks our parents kept us near their sides as though we were five-year-olds. Gradually the nightmare faded and things went back to normal. For a while.

It's Friday, November 22, 1963. Naomi and I are standing waiting for the bus after school. We've just finished writing a history exam and are comparing answers when a girl from our school walks up to us.

"I just heard something amazing from my teacher!"

We hardly know her, so why is she telling us?

"What?" I ask. This is probably some kind of prank. The girl has a weird look on her face.

"President Kennedy was assassinated today."

"John F. Kennedy, the American president?"

"Yup."

"Assassinated?" Naomi gasps.

"Assassinated?" I gasp. Judging from Naomi's expression, I figure it must be something pretty awful.

All the way home on the bus Naomi keeps clucking and I keep right on clucking along with her. When we get to my house I pretend to make a dash for the bathroom, but actually make a dash for the dictionary. *Assassinated.* At last I understand the dreadful news. After all, it's not as though people run around assassinating each other every day. At least in my world they don't.

A few days later we're studying World War I. The teacher talks about the assassination of Archduke Ferdinand, the beginning of that war. Funny, but once you learn a new word it seems to crop up everywhere. Then you can't imagine why you didn't hear tell of it long ago.

7

OUR HOMEROOM TEACHER, Mrs. Evans (otherwise known as Mrs. EE, otherwise known as The Evil Eye), either hates you or she dislikes you — those are the choices. Until recently I was fortunate enough to be merely disliked.

On Monday morning, the week following Kennedy's assassination, we're barely seated at our desks when Mrs. Evans clenches her jaw and scours the room. In The Evil Eye's classroom, there's a Crisis a Day.

"How many people in this class are *left*-handed? Raise your hands." Mrs. EE speaks in *italics*.

Four left arms creep up and up and up.

"Higher! How do you expect me to *see* you? All right, now I want the four of you to remain after school today."

Curiosity and fear are a powerful combination.

I can't imagine what being left-handed has to do with staying after school. I thought detention was a punishment for hoods, guys who light up cigarettes the minute they're off school property. Does writing with my left hand make me part of the criminal element?

For the rest of the afternoon my stomach is tight. I'm supposed to show up at Hebrew school by four o'clock. What am I supposed to tell my Hebe teachers when I straggle in late? What do they know about right-handed versus left-handed? Their days are spent studying holy books.

At last the bell rings. Naomi shuffles by my desk on her way out, offering a glance of pity.

"*Fine*," The Evil Eye begins. "From now on, the four of you will remain after school *every day* until you learn to write with your right hand. It's not *normal* to use your left hand. Later in life you'll be grateful that you can use your right. Pick up your pencil in your *right* hand and let's begin."

Obediently, awkwardly, we grasp our pencils with the right hand. So far, so good. Then she commands us to begin writing. My hand is like a newborn fawn rising to its legs, wobbling and wibbling and uncontrollably jittery. My hand seems to be in the way of the pen as it struggles to move right-bound across the page. I can't do it. The Evil Eye is wild-eyed.

"*Tomorrow*! You'll do better *tomorrow*. And you will stay *every* afternoon until you can do it."

My future looks bleak. Am I going to have to drop out of Hebe while she rehabilitates my brain? Perhaps the Hebe teachers will pity me. Perhaps they'll explain to the class about my handicap and how important it is to handle it now, before I reach adulthood as a permanent misfit. Perhaps they'll even grant special dispensation from test writing....

On the other hand, how would Mrs. EE react if I were to explain that my rehab programme will just have to wait because I can't possibly miss Hebe, not even temporarily? No sooner have I considered that option than I dismiss it.

It is The Evil Eye herself who has made it clear that she has no patience for differences. She has no patience for Jewish kids. She especially has no patience for *left-handed* Jewish kids. If the High Holy Days in September happen to fall on school days, then the Jewish students have to make special arrangements to get their assignments. This makes some of the teachers grouchy. The likes of Mrs. EE take it as a personal insult. In September she had said to me, "Mollie, is it really *necessary* for you to be away again? Don't *your people's* holidays ever end?"

How can an adult, a teacher, not understand Jewish holidays? Aren't adults supposed to know about these sorts of things? I know the inside story on Easter, and Christmas, and St. Patrick's Day, and Shrove Tuesday, and I'm a kid.

"Sorry, Mrs. Evans."

Maybe my humility would erase the furrow from her brow. Or maybe I really did feel sorry, sorry for having disrupted her master plan, sorry for being different, sorry for not realizing that it caused her inconvenience.

"Well, I've had to put up with this *every* year that I've taught. I'm just not certain it's *necessary*." With that she had disappeared in a blaze of chalk dust.

This is madness! I'm seriously thinking of inconveniencing her again by begging off her brain rewiring programme in order to get to *Jewish* school! She would *kill* me, and I mean it in italics.

But then aren't I just as crazy to think that Reverend Bloom, our Hebrew school teacher, would excuse me from Hebe until my brain has been fixed? He's more likely to break his rule of never rapping girls' knuckles with his ruler just to show me up as an example. The way I figure it, it's The Ruler versus The Evil Eye.

All I want is to be Elizabeth Anne — a carefree, right-handed, Christian kid.

Chaim Weizmann look nobly towards the future. These pictures and maps are hung with masking tape which regularly loses its sticking power. When, without notice, they end up slithering down the wall and come to rest on the floor we're always grateful for the diversion.

The windows are bare, so on a late afternoon in autumn when you glance out, all you see is your own reflection against a backdrop of the classroom wall. It's almost impossible to resist smiling at yourself. If you stare hard enough, then you can see beyond your own reflection to the blackness of the alleyway outside.

Before recess is Hebrew language (mainly reading and writing, occasionally speaking), and after recess is Jewish customs, ceremonies, laws and history. It is Mr. Levy who provides the after-recess entertainment. Reverend Bloom is his warm-up act. Reverend Bloom (we call him "Bloomers" behind his back and he knows it, even tolerates it) is more or less the same height as we are and has a thick Yiddish accent — perhaps Polish, perhaps Russian — which feels comfort-able on our ears. Most of our grandparents or par-ents speak with the same accent.

When Bloomers gets angry with us, he erupts like a skullcapped volcano. His black eyes widen to full size, his frenzied eyebrows shoot heavenward, and with his right hand he lifts his skullcap from his wispy salt-and-pepper hair and then plunks it back down. He zooms over to the desk of the offending party and, if it's a boy, clasps his ruler and with his full strength slams that twelve-inch stick across the criminal's knuckles.

"WHAT! Are you CRAZY??" (whack) "Are you a *mishugenah*??" (whack) "THIS is how you act?!" (whack) and so on.

Rumour has it that on occasion blood has flowed. Miraculously, tears never do. Even Dov, who according to the boys is a sissy, doesn't break under the strain. The only thing that breaks is the ruler.

9

T HE EVIL EYE has kept me well past four
o'clock. My late arrival at Hebe causes a stir.
With eyes popping, Bloomers flies towards me as I
enter the classroom.

"Where have you been?" he bellows in an
English that sounds more like Yiddish. "You've
missed a test!" He grabs his skullcap and plops it
up and down several times.

"I ... I ... uh ... I had to stay after school."

"What? What are you talking about? You can't
stay after school. You have to come here. Tell your
teacher. And next time don't talk in class so your
teacher won't keep you after school. Do you hear
me???"

"Yes." I slouch into my desk.

Naomi hands a note to me. Every year she sits
in front of me at Hebe and by now has aced the

behind-the-back, bent-elbow, flipped-up-wrist action that gives the impression that the note-passer is simply scratching her back. I grab the tiny white thing folded in every possible direction until it's the size of a sugar cube.

It reads, "Sorry The Evil Eye is torturing you. Want me to tutor you in right-handed writing? See you at recess. N." Naomi always signs her note "N." just to be certain that I know who penned it. She's very cautious.

Recess is a brilliant invention. Without it, children would shrivel up into quivering nervous little balls. Recess at Hebe has contributed to the survival of the Jewish people. At recess I thank Naomi for her offer, but say that I'll leave the decision about this whole mess to my parents. It feels too big for me to handle on my own.

That night I talk it over with them. When I call them into their bedroom for a moment of private conversation, they know I mean business.

"No," says my mother. "We can't allow this. I don't like to go against what Mrs. Evans thinks is best, but in this case I can't agree with her."

"You mean because I'll miss Hebe?"

"That too. But mainly because I read about this switching idea — it was just a few weeks ago — and they say it can cause all sorts of problems."

"Like red knuckles from ruler-burn?"

"More like stuttering and other things."

My father decides it's time for me to do my homework and time for him to get back to his newspaper.

"Mom will talk to the principal tomorrow about this. So don't worry about it any more tonight."

"But Mrs. Evans will *kill* me if the principal yells at *her* about it."

"I'll make sure that doesn't happen." My mother says this in the kind of voice that makes you feel taken care of by the adults in your life, even though you know in your heart it's about time you fought your own battles.

The next morning comes too quickly as far as I'm concerned. The morning bell rings and we are at our desks by nine o'clock. It's odd that The Evil Eye isn't standing behind her brown wooden barricade shuffling her papers into neat piles. Every morning she performs four rituals: first, paper shuffling, then, glancing up and down the rows of desks sneering, next, straightening her belt so that the buckle is smack-dab in the centre of her waist and, finally, standing erect in preparation for "God Save the Queen."

Where is she today? Has word gotten through to her already? I begin planning my funeral. While the other kids are giddy with dreams of a substitute teacher, I am wondering who will miss me when I'm six feet under.

Just when the first chords crackle through the PA system, The Evil Eye whisks into the room, adjusts her belt and stands erect.

Her face shows no telltale signs. I want the execution to be carried out swiftly. A slow, lingering death is worse. But there is no noose, no guillotine, only the usual miserable face. After all, she *is* only human and therefore entitled to an occasional lapse in punctuality. I begin to relax.

The morning passes without incident until just one minute before mid-morning recess. The principal knocks on our classroom door. The two adults speak in whispers. After recess, The Evil

Eye comes back to class five minutes late (tsk, tsk, late again — doesn't she know that all this tardiness just won't do!). When she finally looks up from her desk, her eyes catch my glance. They grip it until I feel suffocated. This is it. She knows. I am officially demoted from "disliked" to "hated."

10

Each Wednesday in Home Economics we alternate between cooking and sewing lessons. "We" means "girls only." The boys march off to Manual Training where they learn how to use tools for woodworking and metalworking. Apparently females have been cooking and sewing for three million years and we're likely to continue well into the future. Likewise, males have been building one thing or another when they weren't out hunting large game.

Only one girl refused to take Home Ec on the grounds that she wasn't interested. She requested a transfer to Manual Training. The principal granted her dispensation from Home Ec, but kept her from the grubby world of wood and metal shavings. So she spends that one afternoon a week writing book reports instead, and the rest of us envy her.

People seem to be born with a knack for certain skills. One of Naomi's special gifts is her ability to understand the mysteries of food preparation. She has a sense of what to do and why it must be done, and when we have completed our class cooking assignment, Naomi beholds the finished product as a miracle of perfection.

I, on the other hand, behold my finished product as a different kind of miracle. It's shocking to think that anything so unappetizing in texture, appearance and smell could have been created by such a well-meaning individual. For me, food is physical, not spiritual.

That's why I begged Naomi to be my cooking partner when the teacher told us to team up early in the year. At first, Naomi refused to be anywhere within a stove's breadth of me. However, when I mentioned that I might come in handy as her Latin tutor, she saw the light and changed her mind.

"You will bake a cake today, girls." Mrs. Smith's voice is prim and quiet, but everybody listens. "I do not want to hear any talking except whispering with your partner when you need to decide who will do which tasks. You will have thirty minutes to prepare the batter, and then approximately fifty-five minutes to bake it. I have some things to tend to in the office, but I will return when it is time to remove the cakes from the oven. When you've placed your cake in the oven, then I want you to sit quietly and read the article on the many fine uses of gelatin. Now remember, no silliness."

She discusses the specifics of the pound cake recipe and then slips out the door. The back of her sandy brown hair, pulled tightly into a beehive, always reminds me of a hotdog roll.

Naomi draws a huge breath and then sighs one of her mournful sighs. This is because she has to deal with me, her best friend in the whole world, in the kitchen.

"You do as I tell you, okay?" she barks. Who can blame her? Among our gang, my cooking fiascoes are well-known. "You crack the eggs into a bowl and beat them while I measure out the butter and flour."

"But I'm not very good at egg cracking. Maybe you should do it."

"Mollie, you're not very good at ANYTHING in this room so what's the difference? Just do it and don't bug me."

I position myself so that nobody can view clearly what I'm about to attempt. With the glass mixing bowl in place, I hit one egg on the top of it and wait for a crack to appear (in the egg, not in the bowl). Nothing. I try again, this time with more force. Into the bowl tumbles half of the eggshell fractured into tiny shards. Gobs of egg white drool along the side of the bowl — mostly along the outside of the bowl — and onto the counter. By some fluke, I manage to steer the thick yellow yolk into place. It stares up at me, waiting for its brothers and sisters.

But my first responsibility is to retrieve those shell fragments. A spoon seems the logical tool. Each time I come near a piece, it dodges under the spoon and disappears. I decide on the merits of a paper napkin to absorb a smidgen of egg white and with it the surrounding hard specks, but the paper sucks up only the goo and leaves behind the shell. This calls for an age-old solution: fingers. Into the slime they dive. Using my fingertips like spears, I poke at those pesky pieces. They refuse to cooperate. Fine! I think. Who the heck will ever know there are eggshells in this stupid cake!

"All done," I say to Naomi. "What do you want me to do next?"

"Pour the eggs in here."

I do.

"What are those little white things?" she asks.

"I don't know. Let's not worry about it."

She shoots me her look of disgust. "I'm going over to check on the oven. Add the salt and baking powder."

I would have added the salt and baking powder, but just at that moment I have a sudden urge to use the bathroom. I figure those ingredients can wait a minute.

When I get back to the classroom, Naomi is tenderly placing our work of art in the oven. It certainly won't do to tell her about the missing ingredients. The one handy kitchen hint that I *do* know is that baking powder is a "leavening agent." Without it the cake won't rise.

I decide to wait until Naomi is engrossed in her gelatin article before attempting to solve the salt and baking powder situation. After ten minutes she seems sufficiently preoccupied. I slip away from the large table where we read articles and eat our masterpieces, work my way over to the row of hot ovens and peek into ours. Not much action in there. I look in the cupboard for the ingredients and then fumble around for those tiny metal measuring spoons. They're always strung together like keys on a key chain. When you grasp one, the others get jealous and stand up looking for attention too. They all look more or less the same size to me.

When I have measured out the baking powder and salt onto their respective spoons, I open the oven door. I dig a hole, just a small hole, in the top of the cake with my finger. Into it I pour the whiteness of those two magical elements. I feel like Merlin the Kitchen Magician.

Back at the reading table all thoughts have turned to pectin. It is only a matter of time now before Mrs. Smith will return for the coming-out party. Then she will celebrate our talents, and Naomi will be ever so proud of herself and of me. I try to catch Naomi's glance when she looks up from her reading.

"I hope Mrs. Smith likes our cake," I say.

"Why wouldn't she?"

"No reason not to, that's for sure."

Mrs. Smith wafts in through the classroom door.

"Okay, girls. Put down your reading. You will be tested on that next time. Now let's shut off our ovens and remove our cakes. Then we will do a little walking tour and examine each cake."

Perhaps this will be the week that she comes to view me differently, to think of me as something other than a bumbling baker. It's a pleasure to be Naomi's cooking partner; sometimes we work so well together.

"Let's look first at Elizabeth Anne's and Peggy's work ... oh my, how lovely. What a fine texture and colour. You girls clearly knew what you were doing. I like when you people have your wits about you."

Elizabeth Anne grins shyly at me, sharing the pleasure of her success. Even before the school year began she had offered to be my cooking partner out of pity, but I had declined. As sensitive as Naomi is about maintaining her excellent kitchen reputation, Elizabeth Anne is *doubly* so. I couldn't bear to be a regular source of grief for her; somehow I feel Naomi is more used to me, faults and all.

By the time the entire group has shuffled along to our stove, Naomi has begun to dribble tears.

She glares at me as Mrs. Smith frowns a slow, grey frown.

"And what, may I ask, is this supposed to be? Mollie, it's a *pound* cake, not a *pan*cake that I wanted!" The only answer I can come up with is a chuckle of embarrassment.

"Mollie, Mollie! I don't think Naomi finds this funny; do you Naomi?"

"No, Mrs. Smith."

"No, of course not. Now pick up your cakes, girls, and take them home. Each girl gets half."

I turn to Naomi. "Which half do you want?"

"Oh really! I sometimes think that whoever made YOU left out the baking powder."

I suppose I had that coming.

11

Naomi might be the cooking queen, but next to her I'm a regular Olympian in the gym.

The next day, Thursday, we're changing into our glamorous gym uniforms (a bright blue cotton, loose-fitting one-piece affair with short sleeves, big blue buttons down the front, and puffy gathering just above the knees with tight elastic), when Naomi blinks double time and announces, "Mollie, if you don't smarten up in cooking, I'm asking for a new partner."

"You have *got* to be kidding! How can you even think of dumping me? Haven't I improved since last year?"

She pauses, silently bites her tongue, and then bends down to tie the laces on her pure white sneakers.

"Well, haven't I?"

"I suppose, but you do such dumb things. It's like your brain shuts down in that class. How come?"

"I don't know. Everybody is lousy at some things and great at others. Cooking just doesn't happen to be one of my talents."

Her head shakes in mild disgust.

Like every girls' locker room in the world, ours smells like sweaty socks, sweet perfume and clogged toilets. Naomi and I figure we stick out here like sore thumbs. The other girls run around bare naked. Well, some have towels draped over the lower halves of their bodies, but that's where their modesty ends. One girl, Nancy, already uses underarm deodorant. I'm entranced when she performs her hair-brushing ritual in front of the mirror, the way she stares lovingly into her own eyes. After one hundred strokes of the brush, she throws back her head and with a sweep of the hand, flicks the shiny locks from her shoulders.

I wouldn't be caught dead in the nude in front of these people, especially the girls from the other class. And I never would be bold enough to gaze admiringly at myself, even if I were to be filled with admiration. When I watch those girls, I feel puny. When I asked Naomi whether she has any locker room feelings, she told me to stop worrying about such "superficial things." She's probably right.

Miss Clark, the gym teacher, strides into the room. We have five seconds (as measured by her stop watch) to get onto the gym floor. Always "the gym floor." Is this as opposed to the gym ceiling? Would the science teacher ever say, "Now class, you've got five seconds to get onto the science floor."?

The gym is chilly; it feels like a cold echo.

"Two teams for basketball this morning. Line up and call out either 'one' or 'two.' All the ones go over to that corner and the twos over to the other."

There's something so solid about Miss Clark. Even at rest her calf muscles are like India rubber balls. Her orange hair is cut short and to the point. Her cheeks glow red. She wears a shiny silver whistle around her neck that bobs up and down against her tight chest as she marches along. It seems like the only girls in the class whose names she knows are the ones with blond hair, blue eyes, and bulging calf muscles, the ones who look like walking milk commercials. The rest of us annoy her.

Miss Clark blows her whistle.

"Okay. Now girls, listen to me. I want to see some effort out there. I want to see you put your best foot forward. And that includes you, Meredith." Every week she singles out one girl; it's her motivating manoeuvre. When it's my turn, I die a thousand deaths. Maybe if I *had* a "best foot" it wouldn't seem so threatening.

Again she blows her whistle. "Okay. Now move onto the basketball court and wait for the whistle before you begin."

Her whistle shrieks. Lights, camera, action.

Back and forth we run from one end of the court to the other. We're dodging, dribbling, leaping, feeling free. Naomi seems to be out to prove something to herself. She dribbles with the best of them, she leaps as high as she can leap, she even smiles as she plays.

With a magnificent surge, she snatches the ball and begins moving towards the basket. For a split second she stops, and then heaves that ball with the force (and grace) of a bull, and it lands bull's-eye right in the middle of the basket.

She jumps for joy and squeals with sheer delight. She does not sense the rising tide of laughter as it rolls across the gym floor.

All action halts as Miss Clark charges onto the court.

Bleep — bleep — bleeeeep, she blows into her silver necklace.

"Silence, girls! Silence! I will have no more laughing.... Now, you ... what's your name again?"

"Naomi."

"Naomi. What in tarnation do you think you're doing?"

"Sorry, Miss Clark. I don't know what you mean."

"You don't? Then you're worse off than I thought. Which basket is your team's?"

"That one," says Naomi pointing to the correct one.

"And which basket did you put the ball in just now?"

"That one," Naomi says, pointing again to her team's hoop.

Then it hits her right between the eyes. Humiliation spreads throughout her body like a fast-acting rash, and there she stands in front of all of us, even the blond-haired, blue-eyed ones with the calf muscles, there she stands, eyelids fluttering like hummingbird wings.

"Well, Naomi, I thought I'd seen *everything*, but this takes the cake."

Yesterday *my* cake had taken the cake. Now it's Naomi's turn.

Everyone giggles.

I want to reach out to Naomi and shelter her from this moment of rawness, but guilt by association holds me back. She's strong, I figure, she'll cope. She breaks down and weeps and runs from the gym floor and then I follow her into the locker room.

"Don't say a word!"

"Okay."

"I can never show my face here again. I'm going to transfer to another school."

"Okay."

"How was I supposed to know why they were laughing? I've never been that close to the ball before. I thought for once I was as good as anybody."

"You were."

"Then why did I do something so stupid? I feel

like a stupid idiot."

"It was just a mistake."

A powerful force swings open the door. In zooms Miss Clark.

"All right, Naomi, get back out onto that gym floor. And I mean now!" Then she addresses me, "And what are you doing in here?"

"I'm Naomi's friend."

"Look, girls, everyone makes mistakes. But what kind of person are you going to be when you grow up if you can't take a little criticism?"

She glances at us and I think I see a flicker of something — can it be sympathy? — on her face. And then, in a flash of calf, she is gone.

"What kind of person *will* I be?" Naomi honks her runny nose into a tissue.

"A decent one," I say. We return to the floor of the gym together, our own team, indivisible.

12

I MARK OFF MY LIFE in Saturdays. When I dread an upcoming event, such as exams, I count the number of Saturdays until then, and with each one I nod at the passing of time until the wretched event has come and gone. It's the same thing with happy times, like waiting for vacation.

"Mollie, get up. It's time to get up for shul," my mother announces. I open one eye. Saturday again.

Saturday is the Jewish Sabbath. Every Saturday morning my family and I attend services at our synagogue. It's an opportunity to wear nylon stockings plus shoes with a little heel and no shoelaces or straps — an opportunity to escape from brown oxfords. My favourite shul outfit for cold weather is a pink wool sweater set (thin pullover covered with a thin cardigan) decorated at both necklines with tiny white pearls, my A-line grey skirt that stiffly juts below the knee, beige nylons and black pumps.

The entire family looks fresh and rested. My brothers and I are especially nice to each other on Saturday mornings —how can you be mean-spirited when you're all dressed up?

Every Saturday morning while the grown-ups are at the service in the main chapel, Naomi and I and about thirty other kids gather for religious services across the hall in the mini-chapel, a snug room half the size of a regular classroom. The mini-chapel is complete with heavy wooden pews, an ark to hold the Torah scrolls, and yellow stained-glass windows. In fact, most of one wall is long strips of window. On sunny winter mornings they cast an amber glow like corn syrup. This is where we have "Junior Congregation." What makes Junior Cong bearable is the lunch served to the kids downstairs in the auditorium when our service ends.

Mr. Levy, who also teaches after recess at Hebe, stands guard over us during Junior Cong. Like Reverend Bloom's, his temper tantrums are as predictable as the luncheon menu. He places children just slightly above rodents on the scale of animal development. We'd like him if he liked us, but he doesn't, so we don't. It's just as well.

Every few minutes Mr. Levy licks his dry lips as though they're rusty and in need of oiling. He chews his nails up to his knuckles. No one can blame Mr. Levy if he feels more tension and frustration than the average sixty-year-old; after all, he was trained as an accountant. Through a series of unfortunate life circumstances, he has ended up standing sentry over a lower life form.

On Saturdays at noon he distributes salami sandwiches (on fresh chewy rye bread with or without mustard) and soda pop to us. Nothing is quite as satisfying as a salami on chewy rye with mustard and a sip of fizzy pop in a Dixie cup. The experience could be blissful, but Mr. Levy harps from first juicy mouthful to final spicy burp, and he frowns with such contempt that I feel ashamed for taking up his time with an activity as foolish as eating.

His scorn for the chubby is intense.

"He thinks I'm the scum on the underbelly of humanity," Naomi whispers in my ear after swallowing the remains of her sandwich.

"Is this a secret you'd like to share with the rest of us, Naomi?" Mr. Levy snaps. He won't tolerate secrets. And he has a particular dislike for chubby whisperers.

"Not really."

"Not really! Not really!" he apes. Licking his cracked thin lips, he addresses the assembled crowd. "Naomi has a secret she'd like to share with you."

Only the tiniest hint of a burp can be heard.

"Well?"

"I said to Mollie that I think you're handsome."

Flushed, his bony frame slowly turns away from Naomi and heads for the door.

We aren't sure he believed her, but we can predict he'll never again take her name in vain.

13

I T IS SNOWING feather flakes by the time we leave shul. Friends and fellow-sufferers come up to Naomi and congratulate her on her brilliant response. She might not know one end of a basketball court from another, but my friend has a mind and a tongue sharp enough to slice through stone.

After Junior Cong, Phyl, Naomi and I saunter home together. Phyl, nose and hair and all, towers over me in her big-boned glory. Walking beside her I feel protected and small. Nothing too dreadful can happen as long as Phyl is there, busy chatting, busy shocking herself with her own stories. She isn't like Naomi, born on the dark side of the moon where werewolves howl at the black velvet sky.

Phyl's giant clompers leave craters in the snow.

"Want to come to my house this aft?" she asks us.

"I'd like that," Naomi says, "But Mollie and I have to go to Elizabeth Anne's tonight for her birthday pyjama party, so I'll have to go home kind of early to get ready."

"She didn't invite any of the kids from your class, just from our class."

"Oh, that's okay," Phyl reassures us.

"I'll call my mother when we get to your place. What do you want to do?" I ask, knowing full well what she wants.

"Let's watch wrestling." Phyl suggests this with such enthusiam you'd think it's a brand new idea.

"Sure. But I don't like when they slam each other against the floor boards; do you?" Naomi is a pacifist.

"Me neither," Phyl says, but I know she savours these brain-loosening manoeuvres every bit as much as I do.

Soon we're cocooned in her tiny den, venetian blinds down to shut out snow glare and the world. Snug on the brown plaid tweed sofa, we relish the vicious spectacle. The violence is captivating.

"And now, ladies and gentlemen, I give you the

one, the only, the GREAT Bulldog Brown," announces the distinguished sports commentator. Mrs. EE says that a British accent goes a long way in creating the illusion of sophistication.

"I'm HOT today," the Bulldog growls. "He don't stand a chance. I'll break 'im in two like a toothpick." His foaming mouth bites at the microphone.

Suddenly the picture goes topsy-turvy, as if the camera operator were doing cartwheels. Next thing we know the microphone is clutched in the gigantic paw of the ranting, raving Sweet Daddy Sugar. In a primitive voice he grunts something about showing the Bulldog who is boss. Before long these gentlemen are in a full-blown frenzy. The sports commentator manages to break up the fray and to send the opponents to their corners on the boards.

The bell clangs. The men shove one another, yank each other's hair. Bulldog Brown grabs his opponent's arm and whirls him into the ropes. He ricochets onto the floor. Phyl's jaw hangs down. Naomi's eyelids flutter. I peer through fingers spread like a fan across my face. Surely one of them will get killed if this crashing and bashing doesn't stop.

And then Phyl's mother is standing at the doorway, her hair up in rollers. She wears the spongy pink rollers with the pink plastic clasps. It's a tough choice, because the metal rollers with the stiff bristles poking out on all sides (the ones that look like baby porcupines) dig into the scalp, but they don't leave indentations in the hair the way the pink ones do. Phyl's mother explained these differences to us last week.

"Don't you girls have anything better to do?"

"It'll be over soon, Mom."

"I don't understand why you girls watch this stupidity. Why don't you see what's on the other channel, if you must watch at all?"

"There's nothing else on, Mom. The other channel just has a home repairs show now."

"Well, at least it's not all fake, like the wrestling!"

What did Phyl's mother say? All fake?

"What do you mean, all fake?" I ask.

"Haven't you noticed that all the action happens exactly in front of the camera, just at the correct angle? And that no one ever gets hurt? The whole thing is staged; it's a performance."

"You mean like a dance recital?" I want her to

deny this.

"Of course. Because there are people like you three who fall for it, and think it's real, they get away with it. Now shut off the television and go do something useful."

Like three mannequins, we stare stiffly into space. Our silence is broken by Naomi.

"It's better to know the truth about these things."

"Why?" I ask.

"Because it's not good believing things that aren't true."

"Why do you have to be so practical all the time, like a grown-up?"

Phyl intervenes.

"Want some Coke?"

We set aside our differences. Why fight when you can feast on Coke and chips? After a few lazy games of Crazy Eights, a few of Chinese checkers, Naomi and I head for home before the sun goes to bed. Soon we'll be expected at Elizabeth Anne's house.

14

Elizabeth Anne has invited six girls from our class plus two neighbours I've never met before plus her two older sisters, Barbara and Sally. Eleven in all. Actually, Barbara and Sally are more chaperones than guests.

The house is small and cosy. It's a bungalow with a rec room in the basement. The rec room walls are covered with fake wood panelling, the floor with brown linoleum. At one end of the room are a saggy sofa and matching chair, and at the other an ancient piano with several keys silenced by overuse. The guests wander in awkwardly. We all feel shy.

"Okay, girls, let's break the ice with some games!" Barbara tries to get the ball rolling in a voice so perky that Naomi looks at me and rolls her eyes.

No one stirs.

"Don't be shy. Let's start with broken telephone; it's always good for a laugh."

No one moves an inch.

Finally, Elizabeth Anne steps in.

"Why don't we put on a record and listen to some music?"

Everyone agrees. Barbara decides this party is a lost cause and stomps upstairs. We don't see her again.

Elizabeth Anne starts off with a slow velvety number. We unroll our sleeping bags on the floor and prop ourselves dreamily on our elbows. The two neighbours croon along with the record. After we've listened to both sides, someone suggests we switch to Elvis. Elizabeth Anne obliges. Although Naomi continues flipping through the book she brought, everyone else is on their feet, rocking and rolling. We pair off and jive like jumping beans, pushing and pulling and shaking our arms and legs every which way. After twenty minutes we're in a sweaty frenzy. Exhausted, we take a break.

At this point, Elizabeth Anne's parents duck their heads down the stairs and smile a hearty greeting. It's eight o'clock.

"Everything okay, girls? Need a refill on the chips and pop yet?" asks her mother.

"No thanks," we reply in unison.

"It's awfully quiet down there. Are you sure everything's okay?"

"Yup," we reply in unison.

Her parents disappear upstairs, whispering as they go.

Sally, the sister who *hasn't* given up on us, senses our restlessness.

"Why don't we change into our pyjamas? Even though it's still early, it'll feel more like a pj party."

Sounds like a reasonable idea. There's only one problem —where to change. It's one thing to sit next to a person every day in school, to know their most private thoughts, but it's quite another to undress in front of them.

"If you want, you can go up to our bedroom to change," Sally offers.

"Why would we want to do that?" asks one of the neighbours. I can just imagine her prancing around the locker room.

"In case anyone is shy."

"Shy? Changing in front of a bunch of girls?"

Naomi and I take this as our cue and head upstairs for Elizabeth Anne's bedroom. There in the semidarkness we slip into our flannel pyjamas and fluffy slippers.

When we get back, Elizabeth Anne puts on a mellow album and the whole group grows calm. We listen and munch. Conversation begins to flow. It's pretty much the same conversation at every pj party, about our bodies and how they aren't quite what they used to be. Then the neighbour who isn't shy about changing in front of girls makes a confession.

"Want to hear what happened on my date with Richard last night?"

"Yes! Tell us!"

"Well, we were in his car, in the front seat —"

"You go out with guys who are old enough to drive?" someone asks.

"Just this one, just Richard. We've been going together for ages. So we were in the parking lot at Pleasant View Park, the parking lot right down near the water. It was pitch black out and freezing cold, but we had the heat on and we were keeping each other warm...."

I can't believe she's telling total strangers this

level of detail. And I can't wait to hear the rest of it.

"Well, we're listening to music on his car radio and fooling around ..."

"What do you mean 'fooling around'?" someone asks.

"I mean fooling around. Do I have to draw a picture for you? Anyway, all of a sudden someone's shining a flashlight in our eyes. We freeze. I think I'm dead."

She pauses to sip her Coke.

"So then what happens?" we shriek at once.

"I think I'll die. It's the *police*. He shines his flashlight right into our eyes."

The room erupts.

"What did he do?"

"Did he take you to jail?"

"Nah." She takes another sip. "He just told us to go on home."

"Wow!"

Maybe it's embarrassment or maybe it's fear, but suddenly we're laughing our heads off. We laugh and laugh over every little thing for the next four hours. We evaluate every girl in our class who isn't at the party, and every boy. We imitate every teacher except the ones we like. We run up and down the basement stairs making trips to the kitchen for snacks, and while we're up there we run in and out of the bathroom exchanging beauty tips. Even Naomi is giddy.

At one o'clock Elizabeth Anne's father steps into the hallway in his bathrobe and bare feet. His tufty hair is ruffled and his eyes squint against the light beaming from the bathroom.

His voice starts off groggy and builds.

"Girls, if that washroom door slams one more time, if those basement steps creak one more time, if that refrigerator door slams one more time, if I hear one more giggling voice, then I'm SENDING YOU HOME!! NOW!! DO YOU UNDERSTAND???"

We nod meekly and skulk down to the mustiness of the basement. Elizabeth Anne cries softly in humiliation. Sally comforts her. The rest of us crawl into our sleeping bags and pass out, dreaming of boys, cars and police officers with flashlights.

15

CLOUDS HANG HEAVY with snow on Monday when we get out of school at three thirty. By the time we reach Hebrew school, lacy flakes have begun twirling against a white sky. A muffled silence fills the streets, which makes walking sound like tiptoeing on thick carpets. Only a foghorn now and again breaks the spell. Sometimes I think our town is enchanted.

By the time Naomi and I arrive at Hebe, Phyl is already there, busy yanking off her beige snow boots. All the girls in our town wear the same style, same colour: beige rubber, brown fleece lining, a buckled strap around the top of the front to keep it snug. You keep your shoes on and put your snow boots over them. There is one design flaw. A vigorous tug when removing your boot can land you a stockinged foot. In one fell swoop off come boot and shoe, leaving your foot covered in a wrinkled heap of heavy beige stocking clumped around the toes.

Today we somehow manage to keep our shoes on our feet.

Naomi scurries into the classroom and takes her workbooks out of the drawer beneath her seat. She gently places her pencil in the narrow groove designed to hold one pencil and half of one pen at the top end of the desk. There's always something rolling out of that groove, spilling over onto the floor. Naomi places her chubby, well-worn eraser slightly to the right of the pencil and, finally, her wooden ruler stretches its full length just to the south of the groove. She fingers her left braid to make sure it's still neatly plaited and securely fastened, and then she repeats the same exercise with her right braid. At last she opens her workbook to the right page and smoothes it over and over again until it lies perfectly flat. Naomi is a creature of habit. Her rituals comfort her, and watching them comforts me.

"Come to the bathroom with me, will you?" I ask Phyl.

"Sure. You okay?"

"Yup. It's just these stupid stockings. They're always falling down." I hoist them up, first from the ankle and then from the thigh, and reattach them to the four garters that hang from my garter belt. My mother insists that I wear bloomers over the whole works to keep my thighs and tushie from freezing. By the time I get dressed in the morning, I feel like I've put in a day's work.

"How was the pyjama party Saturday? I forgot to ask you yesterday."

"It was great! But listen, was your mother kidding? I mean about wrestling?" I'm hoping Phyl will let me in on the hoax, the big joke played by her mother.

"Nope. She told me she wasn't kidding."

"Oh." I look off at the shiny pink walls. "I guess we'd better get back to the classroom." I'm disappointed, but determined not to be downhearted.

In a heap on the swampy hallway floor lies my heavy, itchy, navy blue woollen coat. I replace it on its hook.

"It doesn't matter," Phyl goes on, "we can still watch it."

"Yup." But I know it will never be the same, at

least not for me and Naomi.

We take our seats just in time to witness Bloomers on one of his rampages.

One of the boys, known to us as Steve by day and Shlomo by late afternoon, has biffed his pink pearl eraser at Dov's head and has landed a bull's-eye.

Bloomers races towards Shlomo, ruler shaking high in the air, whirring with energy.

"Your mother should only know you act like a wild animal!" he screams.

We try to control ourselves, but when he gets to *that* line (which he always does sooner or later), the tittering and note-passing begin. He is power-less to quiet us.

WHACK! WHACK! WHACK!

Shlomo tries to be brave, but this time those whacks bite into his skin. There's a moment of silence while he composes himself.

In disgust, Bloomers lights up the cigarette balancing from his lower lip, dropping its grey ashes onto any victim in its path. Then he stands out in the hallway puffing, probably hoping we'll vanish in a haze of smoke. By the time he comes back to the class, we've wrung the last giggle from ourselves. We're ready to proceed until the next crackdown.

Sometimes we almost feel sorry for him, although I don't know why we should. Kids aren't responsible for adults, are they?

16

SUNDAYS. There's Hebe for two hours. Then weekly skating for an hour at the public arena for the entire Jewish community, both shuls.

"Mollie," my mother calls to me as I'm preparing to leave for Hebe. "Daddy and I want to visit with the Rubins this afternoon. After skating are you planning to go to your Young Judea meeting?" Young Judea is our youth group. It's social, not religious.

"There *is* no meeting this week because of the movie."

My mother looks perplexed. "What movie? Who's showing you a movie?"

"Oh, I guess I forgot to mention it. Through Hebe. All the kids are supposed to meet at two o'clock in the shul gym for a movie called 'Conspiracy of Hearts.' It's something about

Catholic nuns hiding Jewish kids in a convent. Something about World War II. I didn't really understand what Mr. Levy was talking about. But we're supposed to show up. Okay?"

She looks pale. "Do you want to talk a little bit about why nuns hid kids? We can talk about it if you want."

"No," I say as I stroll out of the kitchen, "I'd rather wait and find out when I see it. I don't want to ruin it by knowing ahead of time."

My mother turns back to her baking and opens the oven.

After Hebe we have a quick lunch of waffles and syrup. Then we gather up our ice skates and mittens and all five of us pile into the car. Sunday is the busiest day of the week because we have to go from Hebe to lunch at home to skating to our Young Judea meeting to dinner at home to a hair wash for school the next day to finishing any straggling bits of homework to finally falling into bed. On a good week, when all the tasks are completed by nine o'clock, I get to watch The Ed Sullivan Show with my parents and Norman and go to bed at ten o'clock to read.

Just before two o'clock on this special Sunday, my father drives me to shul for the movie. My father is the family chauffeur. He's quiet, he's punctual, he watches us lovingly from the place where fathers dwell somewhere behind the scenes. But now he seems to need to say something. As I open the car door he takes my other mittened hand and holds it for a quick moment.

"I'll pick you up after the movie. Don't worry. I'll be right here."

"Thanks, Dad. See you."

Why did he say that? Did I look worried? I know he's reliable. Why should I worry? Sometimes adults pop out with the strangest things.

I feel sophisticated arriving all alone for a movie, even if it is just in the shul gym. I've never gone to a movie alone. What would it be like to take a bus to a genuine movie theatre, to buy a ticket, and to sit munching popcorn during a feature film? I don't know whether being alone always means being lonely. I am never alone, not at home, not at school, not even on the way to school and back. There's always someone around. Even when I want a few minutes solo in the bathroom, there's usually somebody banging on the door needing the toilet.

The gym is darkened. At the front of the room on stage is our trusty portable screen, the one they haul out for state occasions. On several rows of metal folding chairs sit almost all of the Jewish kids I know, except of course for the little ones like my brother Ray and the near-adults like my brother Norman. Naomi and Phyl and I sit side by side, silenced by our curiosity.

Mr. Levy ambles up the short staircase beside the stage and stops directly in front of the screen. In the subdued light, framed by a white screen, he looks like a marionette.

"Sit down! This movie is important. It's called 'Conspiracy of Hearts.' It's about a group of nuns in Italy who hid Jewish children during the Second World War so that they wouldn't end up being killed by the Nazis. During the War, twenty million people were killed. Six million of those were Jews from almost every country in Europe."

Did I hear right? Twenty million? Six million Jews? Mr. Levy presses on. For the first time ever, his voice begins to soften. For the first time ever, we listen.

Mr. Levy must be exaggerating. The whole story is too absurd to be true. Grown men murdering babies and grandmothers and grandfathers? What's so special about Jews that we should be chosen for elimination? Nothing makes sense.

The room is now blackened and the movie begins. The kids in the row ahead of us take ten minutes to stop squirming and settle down. I look around to figure out where Mr. Levy is sitting. For some reason, I want the reassurance of his presence. He is in the front row, aisle seat. I slouch in my metal chair and begin to watch.

I cannot believe this story. The plot is impossible. I glance over at Naomi, who's blowing her nose, and then at Phyl, who's wiping her eyes. I can't believe this story.

Finally it ends. I can hear only one sound — saliva rolling down my throat as I desperately try to squelch the tears. Without warning, Mr. Levy flicks on the lights in the auditorium. The contrast stings our eyes. All around me are the faces of well-fed children who have a home to come home to. Had we been born ten years earlier, or even five or six years earlier, and had we not been separated from that inferno by the ocean ... Time and

Place. Place and Time. The right Time and the right Place, or the wrong Time and the wrong Place, that's what it boils down to.

I jump up from my metal chair, trip over Phyl's feet, then over Naomi's, run upstairs and out through the heavy front doors. There is my father in the car, waiting for me. I throw myself into the seat beside him and weep until his heart breaks.

17

F OR DAYS THE SIMPLE acts of daily living take on a new texture. I am grateful to have food, to have a toothbrush with toothpaste, to have clean sheets, to have parents. Everything about my parents seems sweet. I feel tenderness towards Norman and Ray. I want them to understand, but there are no words in my mouth. The words are trapped in my heart.

How can I have been alive all these years and not known about this Thing? There are probably people in my own shul who survived It, even in my own family. It takes me until Wednesday night during supper to dare to raise the topic.

"My mother and father lost brothers and sisters and their children and some cousins. They were from Lithuania." That is all my father says at first.

Quickly I calculate. These had been my great-aunts and great-uncles and distant cousins. For the few years that I'd known my father's mother, I'd never known the most tragic fact about her life. She hadn't walked around crying. She didn't even seem sad. If my family were killed, I'd never stop crying, not for one minute as long as I lived.

"There are several members of our shul who are survivors of the concentration camps." My mother picks up from where my father leaves off. "Many have numbers tattooed on the under part of their forearm. People in some camps were assigned numbers and branded like cattle. The tattoo is a fleshy memory." She goes on to list at least five people I know. I'd never noticed the smooth underbelly of their forearms. I'd never noticed anything unusual about them.

I'd never noticed anything. I'd spent all my life in a fog. Suddenly the mist is lifting and I'm left staring at a strange land. Nothing is familiar.

"What about if you gave up being Jewish, if you promised the Nazis you would convert to another religion? Would they leave you alone then?"

My father almost smiles at me. "No, they wouldn't leave you alone. If you were born a Jew or even had any Jewish blood in you from previous generations, then you were defined as a Jew and destined for death."

"So if the Nazis decided you didn't fit with their idea of a perfect person with the right blood and looks and everything, then nothing could change their minds?"

"Right. They made the decisions about who fit in, the life or death decisions."

I hate that other people can decide on what sets you apart, what it is about you that makes you different, what it is about you that should count the most. It isn't fair.

On Saturday morning I decide to leave the Junior Cong lunch as quickly as the Law of Levy allows and join my mother in the main chapel. My father sits in the men's section, just an aisle separating us.

One of the survivors my mother had mentioned was Mrs. Farb. She is just two seats away, just the distance of a furtive glance to the left of my mother's seat. But it is long-sleeve weather, not the season for bare forearms. This calls for a plan, a scheme.

I like Mrs. Farb. She's one of those adults who is jolly and modern and always interested in what young people think. How could she have ... ?

"Hi, Mrs. Farb," I whisper, leaning across the empty seat between us.

"Hi, *shana madel*, my beautiful girl," she replies, eyes smiling, her deep red lipstick accentuating the gold-capped tooth just to the right of centre. I think of Nazi soldiers ripping out gold teeth to melt them down....

"I like your bracelet," I whisper back. "May I see it?" She signals for me to move into the seat next to her. I tell Mom I'll be back in a jiffy as I manoeuvre into position beside Mrs. Farb. She holds out her arm; her sleeves are long, but loose. I begin to blush. What if she sees through my scheme? What if she explodes with outrage at my insensitivity? What if she tells my mother?

"Here, *shana madel*, here. Take it off. Go ahead. Try it on yourself. Don't be shy."

There is her arm, in front of me, an invitation to peek beneath the sleeve, to bear witness to her tragedy. I fumble with the bracelet clasp, but my fingers shiver.

"Oi, this crazy thing. It's such a nuisance.

Here, let me do it."

She bends over her own wrist to tackle the jewellery. After fiddling for a moment, she pushes her sleeve up her arm as if to clear away the mess, to make room to work.

My breath sucks into my throat with such force that Mrs. Farb's eyes turn to meet mine. Those digits, in blue. My eyes dart to my lap. Then to my mother. Then to my lap again. Then they stop running away and give themselves over to Mrs. Farb. She feels sorry for *me*. Oh please God, please erase this whole scene. Please make Mrs. Farb not know what I'm thinking and feeling. Please don't let her understand. Please don't let her know why I'm crying.

"*Shana madel*," she croons as she rolls down her sleeve. "Wipe your eyes. Give me a smile."

I lick the tears that are dribbling over my top lip and make a feeble attempt at a smile. My mother hears my gulping. The two women exchange glances.

18

"NAO, I NEED TO TALK to you," I speak softly, almost secretively, into the telephone receiver. "It's about the movie we saw last week at shul."

"What about it?" Naomi sounds almost flat, distant.

"I can't get it out of my mind. What about you?"

"I've thought of it."

"Do you think it could happen again? I mean, could it happen here, to us?"

"I don't know. I guess it can happen anywhere if people let it happen."

"Well, aren't you worried about it?"

"Mollie, I'm not going to walk around worrying about being killed because I'm Jewish. I've got other things on my mind."

"But aren't you upset about what Mr. Levy told

us, the part about the kids being separated from their parents?"

For a few seconds the only sound I can hear is Naomi's breathing. Then she speaks.

"Of course I'd hate that more than anything in the world. My mother ..."

"What about your mother?"

"Um ... my mother always says 'why borrow trouble?'"

"I suppose ... but isn't it a shock, I mean the whole thing, the dead babies and everything...."

Silence. Then the slight sound of sniffling.

"Nao, are you okay?"

More silence.

Then, "Okay?! Of course I'm not okay. You call me and remind me of dead babies and being separated from my parents and then you expect me to be okay?"

"Sorry. I guess I just needed to find out what you were thinking because I can't get it out of my head. It's so hard for people to talk about. Even Mr. Levy hasn't said a word all week. I just needed to talk and who else would I want to talk to but you?"

"Well, thanks Mollie; I mean for choosing me.

But I can't say anything more now. Okay?"

"Okay," I say. "See you tomorrow."

When I hang up the receiver my mother comes by.

"Are you feeling okay, Mollie?"

"Sometimes Naomi is so weird. I was trying to talk to her about that movie we saw, and she kept avoiding it."

My mom is quiet for a moment. She touches my hair.

"Maybe it was too sad for her to think about, or at least to talk about," she says and walks into the livingroom.

I stroll by and take a head count. Mother, father, two brothers — everybody in their place and accounted for.

19

SOMETIMES I FEEL like a stranger inside my own body. My body seems more grown up than my thoughts. Friday comes and I feel like playing like an innocent little kid. The wrestling business, the movie, have jostled me more than I care to admit. Naomi agrees to come over after school. Maybe she's feeling the same way.

Last week we saw an educational film at school, a National Film Board documentary about the construction of an igloo by a father and son team. Naomi and I decide we're keen to try our hand at igloo building. It looks so simple, so methodical, so repetitive.

Soon it will be the shortest day of the year. We turn on the light above my back door. Northern Lights. We are the parents. We tramp across the frozen tundra. At last we find the perfect spot for our new home. We set to work in the semidarkness shaping snow bricks.

Within minutes our mittens are stretched two sizes bigger than usual, studded with gobs of ice. Our fingers ache. But our children need us to complete the task lest they be found frozen on the dog-sled by morning. Next door, the dog's whimpers warn of tragedy to come.

"Nao, this snow isn't sticking together."

Naomi wipes her nose with her mitten. "We need wet snow."

My arms feel like they're yanking out of their sockets.

Naomi looks at me. The light from the back door seems weaker. Everything aches — my toes, my fingers, my nose. I wonder how long I can go on.

We add a few more blocks, but they keep sliding off. At last Naomi stops.

She swallows hard. "I'm sorry, but I think our children are going to die from the cold. We can't seem to build a proper home for them."

"Oh, that's okay, Nao. At least the parents are still alive."

"But why would parents want to be alive if their children are dead?" She asks this question as though she wants an answer.

"Gee, I've only thought about it the other way around. I ... I can't imagine what I'd do if ... if my mother and father were taken away from me for some reason."

"I can't either," Naomi says in a quavering voice.

She's standing with her back to the Northern Lights. I can faintly make out her black eyes piercing that wedge of space between the top of her scarf wound round her nose and mouth, and her frozen bangs. Her eyes are moist.

"I'm going home," she says. She says it with as much dignity as she can muster.

"You mean you're quitting?" Of course she's quitting. For goodness sake, she's even crying. "Are you crying, Nao?" Of course she's crying. She always cries when she's frustrated. Her eyelashes are fluttering double time. But this is more than frustration, there's something more here I don't understand. And then she's gone, without another word.

I love one hundred things about Naomi, but sometimes I just don't understand her. I guess you can love someone and not completely understand them.

20

S ANTA CLAUS IS COMING to town. Christian kids
have to worry about whether they've been
naughty or nice. I figure Jewish kids are off the
hook.

The pre-Christmas season can awaken every
one of your senses. There's the sight of a stray
strand of tinsel captured in the frozen sidewalk,
there are the cheerful voices of usually serious
adults, and the sweet stickiness of well-sucked
candy canes glued to soggy cellophane wrappers. I
have to admit there are things I love about it: the
fresh fragrance of Christmas trees for sale propped
against wooden fences, the feel of velvet party
dresses prettily displayed in the shops.

All that aside, I am grateful to be past the age
of public school Christmas concerts. It would start
in November. Teachers launched preparations,

sewing costumes with wings sprouting from the back, constructing rickety manger props, and making students practise carols until they could be sung "with feeling." I was never sure just which "feeling" the teachers meant. For me, guilt and awkwardness were the main sentiments. This was probably true of the other Jewish kids in my class, but we never compared notes. When you're squirming inside your own skin, you don't feel like confessing it to too many people. You figure you're the only one who feels that way.

The confusion can be counted on each hand. On the one hand, preparing a performance for parents is exciting, plus carols (when sung with feeling) sound so sweet, plus wearing a costume is thrilling (even if it's only as one of many jolly Christmas trees), plus having your parents beaming up at you from the audience makes you feel especially loved (it's one of those rare times when you get to see your parents as just general members of the public, separate from you, and you feel proud of the way they measure up next to the other parents), plus if you refused to be in the concert what would you do for half a month, plus, once again, you'd stick out, you'd be different.

Then there is the other hand. Pretending even for one evening that you're Christian and that Baby Jesus is your Saviour feels strange, like being a traitor to your religion, plus what if our Hebe teachers found out, plus what if God found out, plus how can you ever help your friends understand that Jews aren't some form of Christian if you walk around singing "Christ is born in Bethlehem?"

So between the two hands, there's a lot of deep confusion. And it isn't made any easier by the fact that Christmas and Chanukah usually fall within a few weeks of each other, and both teachers and friends insist on referring to Chanukah as "your Jewish Christmas." The conversation usually goes like this:

"Mollie, what are you getting for Christmas from your parents?"

"We don't celebrate Christmas. Remember?"

"Oh, right, I forgot. How come?"

"We're Jewish and Jews don't have Christmas."

"But you have your Jewish Christmas, right? What's it called again?"

"You mean Chanukah. But Chanukah isn't our Christmas because it has nothing to do with Christ."

"You mean you don't believe in Christ as your Saviour?"

"Nope."

"You mean you really don't believe in Christ??"

"Nope."

"Oh. Well anyway, I hope you have a Merry Christmas."

"Thanks."

It's strange that people can think Jews are simply a quirky version of Christians.

Discussion around the family dinner table about the upcoming Christmas concert was always full of the one hand and the other hand. My parents were careful not to force me in either direction. Norman had walked the same fine line in his day, and Ray is sure to benefit from our experience.

"I know the answer," I would conclude each time. "I'll just mouth the words. That way I can be in the concert, but without really saying the words."

Truth is, I never cared what the concert represented. What mattered most was that I didn't have to stick out, I didn't have to be different. I could be a little Jewish Christmas angel, plain and simple. All I wanted then was to fit in. Now I'm not so sure what I want. Now nothing seems so plain and simple.

21

CHRISTMAS MORNING 1963 dawns crisp and white. Every year I feel the same way on Christmas morning — empty, like a vacant lot.

By December 25th the hubbub has ended. A blanket of silence is spread over everything. Even the memory of what I learned in the movie has been laid to rest, at least temporarily.

I'm in the mood to chat with Elizabeth Anne, but there's no point in phoning her. No doubt she's sitting around the family tree watching its lights blink, its baubles clink. She and Barbara and Sally exchange angora sweater sets in powder blue or baby pink or even red. Her dad smiles at his offspring, calmly smoking his aromatic pipe. He is toastily wrapped in his new heavy-knit cardigan: an oatmeal shade with delicate snowflakes running down the front. Elizabeth Anne's mom has secretly been knitting it since early October. The family dog, a shaggy yet endearing little creature, lies contentedly yawning and licking his chops. Elizabeth Anne's mother is in the kitchen, a Christmas apron tied around her waist to protect her skirt from cranberry splashes and turkey grease.

Just before lunch time, Uncle Jim and Aunt Kathy arrive, as they do every year. Then another round of gift exchanging occurs. So the day goes, with family and friends coming and going, each wearing a bright new sweater, bearing gifts and savoury foods. The three sisters are perfectly polite towards one another. Elizabeth Anne's parents are so gracious, even when the dog throws up the half-digested tree ornament. Their world is like a warm embrace.

Or so I imagine.

On our street just a few cars tiptoe by. Usually it's a main thoroughfare for buses and trucks. There is a constant buzz of traffic, of honking and brake-screeching. There are people passing by on their way to the grocery store down the street, children racing by on their way home from school. It's not a street of tranquillity; for our city, it's a beehive. But on Christmas Day, I feel stranded, almost panicked at the thought that the city has closed down. What if I need to buy something? (Although I can't imagine what, since the only thing I ever buy is my favourite slab of toffee and I've got a week's supply of that stashed away.)

Every year it gets harder to spend the entire day with my family, especially when the outside world has vanished. It's not that they aren't a fine bunch; it's just embarrassing. Naomi, my only hope of salvation, is off to Montreal for the holiday to visit her aunt and uncle. Traitor!

Mrs. EE instructed us to write a report during our Christmas break. She said to look at our family, to describe their appearance, their language and their behaviour as though we were aliens from Mars. "Point out everything about them that seems peculiar to you."

On Christmas Day, lonely day, non-Christian day, it's an easy homework assignment for me. Everything about my family seems peculiar. Unlike Elizabeth Anne's family, unlike the whole rest of the world, there's no tree, no father decked in pipe and cardigan, no mother whistling carols in the kitchen, no dog, no shortbread in the shape of Christmas trees with little green sprinkles on them. Instead there is my father in freshly ironed white shirt reading the newspaper, my mother listening to opera on the radio, plucking pinfeathers from the kosher chicken, Norman reading a science magazine on his bed, Ray playing with toy cars on the kitchen linoleum, no pets except for a dopey turtle that can't even race in a straight line, all of them unaware that I am observing, comparing, wishing that we didn't have to be different. Just for once, I want someone to envy my holidays. No Christian kid ever sat around wishing she could celebrate Rosh Hashanah, the Jewish New Year.

I dash to the phone on the second ring.

"Hello," I puff, thankful to have been shaken from my poisonous thoughts.

"Hi Mollie." Elizabeth Anne speaks so gently. She never raises her voice.

"Oh, hi Elizabeth Anne. How come you're calling? I mean, aren't you busy on Christmas Day?"

"Yes, but I just had to get away from my family for a while. My mom was screaming at us all day yesterday 'cause she said we never help her when company's coming. And you know my dad. He thinks his jokes are hilarious. My family really bugs me sometimes. Know what I mean?"

I don't know whether to laugh or to cry.

"So how many angora sweater sets did you get?" I ask.

"Angora sweater sets?!"

22

E VEN BEFORE THE Christmas holidays began I'd been missing Naomi. We hardly ever go more than twelve hours without talking to each other. Our evening phone conversations about homework, clothes, friends, teachers and certain boys (not necessarily in that order) usually last longer than our parents feel is reasonable, although I'm certain that if they knew what we were discussing, they'd feel differently.

Sometimes we talk until our throats are sore. My father says that if anyone ever did try to get through to our house in an emergency, they'd give up and die. He touches the telephone receiver when I hang up the phone.

"A person could burn his hand on this thing."

"One day her ear will fall off," my mother chimes in.

"Ha, ha!" They think they're pretty funny.

For the two nights before Naomi left for Montreal, she was "unable to come to the phone," according to her brother Moe. What could she possibly be doing that was so important, so gripping? Could it be that each time I phoned she was on the toilet?

"Moe, what do you mean? Is she sick or something?"

"No. She's just busy." Moe is tense and surly, as though everyone is out to hurt him and he'd better protect himself before they succeed.

"Um. Oh, I see. Um. Well, would you ask her to call me when she's not busy?"

"Okay," he says, slamming down the receiver.

The night before we return to school, I want to take Naomi's emotional pulse. We haven't spoken since before she went away and now I want to know whether she's as nervous about going back to school as I am. Any Monday morning is nerve-jangling, but at the end of a holiday I can barely imagine conforming to the routine. The move from the gentleness of home to the cruelty of The Evil Eye seems impossible. I want to fly back to my nest where I'm accepted and loved unconditionally (usually). At the very least, I want the company of Naomi's misery.

I phone her place. I dial each number slowly and deliberately, waiting for the metal plate with the finger holes in it to spro-i-ng back to position zero before placing my finger in the hole for the next digit. Naomi's phone number is synonymous with her name.

Her sombre "hello" jars me.

"Why do you sound so weird, Nao?"

"Do I?" is all she says.

"Want to talk about tomorrow?"

"Sorry, Mollie, but my dad needs the phone now. He wants me to get off. Sorry. See you in the morning."

She sounds as distant, and as muffled, as a foghorn far out at sea. I am standing on the shore, hoping the fog will lift by morning.

23

"YOU SEEM DIFFERENT, Nao. What's bugging you?" It's our first lunch hour back at school and we're strolling around the school ground, stretching our legs.

Naomi's eyelids flutter.

"Aren't you going to tell me?"

"I can't tell you. My parents said I couldn't tell anyone." She looks down at a sheet of paper-thin ice that lightly conceals a puddle. Her eyes are glistening the way they had the afternoon of our failed igloo.

"You can tell *me* though. I'm your best friend."

What can be so private that a whole family keeps it secret? Maybe it's about money. I know my parents never want us to discuss "private business" outside our home, which is no problem for me since I don't know any. Maybe Naomi's father

24

WHEN YOUR BEST FRIEND isn't behaving like a best friend, you scrounge around for scraps of love wherever you can find them. At first you discover lovely tiny tidbits about your second and third best friends that you would never have bothered searching for had your best friend not stopped behaving like one. You feel almost freed from your best friend.

But with time, and usually not much time, the excitement fizzles. There are reasons why your third best friend was not and never will be your best or even second best. You are haunted by memories of special moments spent in friendship with your Best.

On Friday I make one last-ditch effort to interest Naomi in joining me at the plaza for a pistachio experience.

"Sorry, Mollie. I promised my mother I'd help her with dinner."

"But you never help her with dinner, even on Fridays. Why today?"

"Because she wants me to start doing more around the house. She ... she says it's time I learned."

"My mother says that every day, but she doesn't really mean it."

"Well, my mother does really mean it."

"Otherwise would you have come with me to the plaza?"

Naomi radiates a warmth that I haven't felt from her in far too long.

"Yes, otherwise, yes."

I am determined to turn my thoughts away from Naomi. I'm even weary of the same old routines with Phyl and Elizabeth Anne. Sometimes a person needs a change of scenery. Sometimes a person needs to forget that dreadful things have happened in this world and probably will happen again.

Not since the final days of summer have I spent time with my next-door neighbour Kelsey and the other neighbourhood kids, Betty and Chris. They attend a nearby Catholic school, so our paths cross mainly when spring draws us outside. Since we were little we've been skipping together, and bouncing our India rubber balls against the walls of our houses, and fighting about everything under the sun. Kid stuff. There's always an unspoken distance between us, but the convenience more than makes up for the lack of depth.

Kelsey's so beautiful, so smooth and delicate in the way Phyl had described the girls at public school. In the summer her tawny skin glows and her pale blue eyes of winter become summer turquoise and her white teeth sparkle. It's as though every part of her is perfectly planned. I would feel quite plain, or even ugly, next to Kelsey, if she didn't have her special way of showering sweetness on everyone near her.

After wolfing down some milk and chocolate chip cookies, I walk next door to pay a visit to Kelsey.

"Hi, Mollie! I haven't seen you in a dog's age."

"Want to do our telephone thing?" I ask, figuring this will break the ice.

"Uh, sure, I guess so."

"You dial," I order, handing the telephone to her.

"No, you. You're better at this."

"Okay, but tell me if your mother's coming." I dial seven digits chosen at random.

"Hello," the woman says.

"Hello," I reply in my most mature voice. "Is your fridge running?"

"Why, yes," the woman says.

"Oh, then you'd better go and catch it!" I crash down the receiver.

"It worked! It worked! That woman said 'Why, yes.'"

We cackle, hovering between guilt and the thrill of being publicly naughty. Sometimes you need a break from acting your age. With all that has been going on, I feel entitled to a few moments of goofiness.

Soon it's time for me to go home for supper. I never stay for supper at Kelsey's house. No one stays. I would though, if I were invited.

Their place is more like a low-ceilinged cottage than a city house, and into it they squeeze Kelsey's mother, her father, who wears an army uniform, her Granny, who shares Kelsey's bed, her

Uncle Bill, who never seems to walk straight, her handsome older brother who yearns to be a priest, her younger brother and sister, and their dog Blackie.

Some nights I hear Blackie whimper outside their back door. At long last, Kelsey's mother opens the door. Breaking the silence of the cold night air, as though Blackie were deaf, she trumpets "Blackie, Blackie, come in girl." Blackie shuffles the three or four steps to the door (paint-peeled wood on the bottom half, torn screen on the top half). Then sounds of claws are heard scuttling over the kitchen linoleum, and at last the door slams shut. Kelsey's mother and father are calling it a night.

I would stay there for supper, but I guess there isn't any room. There's no room and there's probably not much extra food for guests. I notice for the first time today that their house is cold and sort of ramshackle. There's no fruit bowl brimming with crunchy apples and juicy oranges, not a hint of luxury. For the first time I realize Kelsey's family must be poor.

25

AFTER SHUL THE next day, both Naomi and Phyl have plans. Naomi, who never has plans other than with me, suddenly has plans. And Phyl has to spend the afternoon with her grandparents. I decide to knock on Kelsey's door again.

A fried bacon aroma permeates the faded roses on the wallpaper just inside the entrance way; it permeates every ramshackle inch of that house and gives the impression that Kelsey and her family are forever eating breakfast.

"Hi stranger," Kelsey's mother smiles.

"Is Kelsey home?"

"Yup, she's out back. So's your friends Betty and Chris. Go ahead. Go round back."

She shuts the door behind me and I slide across the snow drifts, now hardened into ice drifts, that fill the space between Kelsey's house and mine. Before I reach the backyard I hear laughter.

I feel almost shy seeing Betty and Chris again after such a long time. Chris is a year older and bolder than the rest of us. Betty is like a handmaiden to Chris. She dotes on her and obeys her. No one would ever accuse Betty of being smart.

"What did you get for Christmas, Mollie?" Betty shouts through the cold moist air floating from her mouth in a lingering, puffy cloud.

THAT question again. My heart sinks.

"I didn't get anything," I answer in a voice meant to curry sympathy and at the same time to ward off further questions.

"Why not?"

"Remember? I explained this last year. We don't believe in Jesus. Don't you remember?" I can't stand the thought of reviewing it again. Why are some differences so difficult to grasp?

"Oh yeah, I forgot. I forgot you're Christ-killers."

"What? What do you mean?"

"We learned it in school. You people killed Jesus. That's why you don't believe in Christmas."

"You learned that in school?" The hairs on the

back of my neck stand at attention. Is it possible that we are guilty as charged? "Is that really what they teach you in Catholic school? I don't believe you. And besides, your mother always says hello to my mother on the street. Why would she do that if she really thought my mother was a Christ-killer?" My voice quivers. I don't know which is worse: the fact that Betty is rejecting me or the fact that Betty is accusing me of a crime which, to the best of my knowledge, had been committed almost two thousand years before I was born.

Chris is happy to join in a good tongue-lashing. Until now she has been silent, looking angelic as the winter rays shoot golden arrows through her long straight hair.

"Betty's right. Our priest said the same thing. He said Jews don't read the New Testament and they think they're the Chosen People, like they're special or something. And my parents told me Jews are rich but cheap."

"How 'bout you, Kels?" Betty asks.

Kelsey frowns. She seems pained, trapped.

"Well, I learned the same things at Catholic school, but my mother said she thinks Mollie and her family are good neighbours and really kind and everything, and so she said you can't just say all Jews are rich or cheap because Mollie isn't rich or cheap. So I don't know really."

Chris and Betty are disappointed in Kelsey.

"I'm going home," Chris announces.

"Me too." Betty follows Chris over the laneway ice drifts out onto the sidewalk in front of Kelsey's house. Their snickers waft towards the backyard.

"Sorry," I say to Kelsey before I drag myself away. Just like with The Evil Eye, there it is again — sorry.

26

BACK HOME I can breathe again.

Looking up from her magazine, my mother distractedly mumbles, "Have fun, dear?"

"No!"

"What happened?"

"I just learned that Jews are Christ-killers."

"What are you talking about? Who told you that?"

"My 'friends.' Chris and Betty."

"Oh, them. People can learn to hate if they don't hear differently at home."

"Kelsey isn't like them."

"Kelsey's parents are kind people, good people. What did Kelsey say when they were calling you names?"

"She sort of stuck up for me."

"Well, that's something. Good for her. I'm sure

it wasn't easy for her. What did *you* say when your friends insulted you?"

"I don't remember. It's sort of a blur. I can't believe they learn those things at school too. I'm going to call Elizabeth Anne to ask whether she hears the same stuff at her church."

"Okay, but go easy."

"What do you mean?"

"I mean, try not to get too worked up with Elizabeth Anne. What your friends said to you isn't right, but it isn't Elizabeth Anne's fault. I doubt very much that she agrees with them."

My fingers are shaking as I dial her number.

"Elizabeth Anne," I get right to the point, "has your minister ever talked about Jews in his sermons?"

"Uh ... um ... uh ... why do you ask?"

"Has he?"

"Well, sort of. I mean nothing much. He sometimes talks about people who don't believe in Christ as our Saviour. I think he feels sort of sorry for people who don't believe. But I don't think he ever said anything bad about them, if you know what I mean."

"Do you feel sorry for me because I'm Jewish?"

"No, not really. If that's what you believe in, then it's fine with me."

"Do you ever feel that we're different because we don't have the same religion?"

There's a long pause on the line. A queasy, empty sensation begins to flutter in my stomach. Finally Elizabeth Anne draws a breath and begins to speak.

"I guess I do feel we're a bit different. It's not so much you and me, it's more other Jewish people I know. They do seem to act ... uh ... well, maybe different than my family."

"In what ways do you mean?"

"It's hard to say. They just seem to treat their kids ... well, like they're more ... they just seem more involved or something. Closer. Like the parents know what's going on more, they drive them places more.... The kids tell their parents things that I would never tell my parents and ... oh, I don't even know what I'm saying. It's just that there is something about Jewish people that's unusual if you're not one of them."

"I see." I don't see at all. I can't tell whether I've been insulted or not. I don't know what to say.

"Mollie, I don't mean any harm by what I've

said. I like Jewish people. They're always really kind to me. And of course you're one of my best friends. And I think your parents are really great."

"Can I ask you a question?"

"Okay."

"How come when I visit your house and your mother is on the phone, she'll say to whoever she's talking to: 'Mollie is over; she's Elizabeth Anne's little Jewish friend.' Why does she describe me like that?"

"I'm not sure. I guess you're different than most of the kids who come over here. I can't answer your question. Do you want me to ask my mother?"

"No. Definitely not. Do you think we could ever be best, best friends even though we're not the same?"

"I don't know. I suppose so, but it's just that I feel you're sort of mysterious in a way, even though I know so much about you. Like when you have a Jewish holiday, it always seems so full of unknown pieces. I feel as though you belong to a secret club I can never join."

"A secret club??"

"That's sometimes how you make me feel, as

though I can't join your secret club. You even learn a code language at Hebrew school so no one else can understand what's going on there. We're not like that; you could come to our church and understand everything right away. It's not like we're trying to keep you out. But I sometimes feel kept out of your world."

"I didn't know you felt that way. I don't do it on purpose."

"Yes, I know. It's not you. It's your whole community."

"Gee, I'm really sorry. Want to come to synagogue with me some day?"

"Maybe. I don't know how my parents would feel about that. I could ask them."

"Want to come over for Friday night dinner sometime?"

"Maybe. I might feel strange. I wouldn't know what to do."

"There's not much to know. We say a few prayers over the candles and the bread and the wine and then we eat. It's not that complicated really."

"We'll see."

"You really are uncomfortable, aren't you?"

"I'm sorry, Mollie. I don't mean to make it sound that bad. It's just that you're putting me on the spot, asking these sorts of questions. Isn't it enough that we're good friends? Why do you have to bring in all these other things? Can't we just have fun together and you do whatever you want in terms of religion and I'll do what I want and that's that?"

"As long as I don't need to feel that you're judging me because I'm Jewish."

"No, I'm not judging you, honest. You're one of the best friends I've ever had."

"You too."

"Thanks."

There is a shadowy tension, as though each of us is trying too hard to be polite. The thought of seeing her at school on Monday sets my butterflies a-flying.

27

I'M FEELING more confused than ever and hungry to be with Naomi. But the next morning at Hebe she pretends to be too involved in the pursuit of knowledge to acknowledge my pursuit of her.

Later I hobble by her at the usual Sunday family skating session at the arena. My ankles meet in the middle as they scrape along the ice. My shins ache.

"How come your mom isn't here to watch you?" I'm desperate for her to bare her soul, to cough up all the words that have been choking her.

"She couldn't make it." Naomi stares at the ice. She wobbles her way to the opening in the boards and up onto the bleachers where Moe is talking with a friend. She doesn't come back.

Bleakness. That big old barn of an arena paints pictures of gloom. Most weeks the skating music lilting through the sound system stirs up special things in me. I become someone else, someone far more lovely, far older. But this week the music grates. I don't feel like imagining romance when I feel such hurt, such confusion. My parents and brothers are skating and smiling.

Someone taps me on the shoulder. It's Crazy Louie. Some folks say he got that way because he bumped his head on a radiator as a baby; others claim he fell out of an airplane when he was in the Air Force during the war and his parachute failed to open.

"Hi," Crazy Louie beams. He might be crazy, but at least he's friendly. "You sure have a pretty mother. She's the best lookin' woman in town. I would've married her, but your dad beat me to it." And off he skates. Every week, Crazy Louie taps me on the shoulder and repeats those exact same words. At first I was afraid of him, but when my mother laughed at my story, I relaxed. Now skating wouldn't be the same without him.

Nor would it be the same without Mr. Shapiro's Juicy-Fruit gum. He's a crackerjack skater. He twirls forwards and backwards, and hands out a stick of gum to every kid. He flashes his broad white smile, gliding past each child, depositing one foil-wrapped stick per kid into their mittened fists. When you no longer get a piece, you know you've passed from childhood. On days when he happens to have a few extra slices, he'll give them to me and Naomi, and in the twinkling of a skate blade we're seven-year-olds again. If only this were one of those days.

My parents are across the rink chatting with friends. They seem so young when they're out in the world, not burdened with whatever it is that makes them old when they're at home. Out in the world they seem more carefree than I do, and they make me think people in the old days really knew how to have fun.

After an hour in that drafty ice rink watching others like a spy behind an open newspaper in a hotel lobby, wondering just exactly where I fit in, if anywhere, I am ready to go home. More than ready.

28

PAPRIKA AND ONION waft towards me in the livingroom. The Friday night chicken and potatoes are roasting, unaware of the fate that awaits them. It has been a week since I've spoken more than a few words to Naomi. She seems to be slipping through my fingers.

I stretch out on the couch and stare at the design of plaster swirls in the ceiling. Then I hang my head sideways off the couch until I'm almost upside-down. I imagine what it would be like if the ceiling were the floor. You'd have to step up over the door frame to enter the room. The light fixture would be the decorative centrepiece. Other than that, there would be no furniture cluttering the floor.

The phone rings. I tumble off the couch and land facedown on the carpet. Too lazy to stand up,

I crawl the few yards to the telephone table.

"Hi, Mollie. It's me. Are you going to shul tomorrow?" It's Phyl. I'd been hoping it would be Naomi calling to beg me to get together after shul for a wild game of Chinese checkers, calling to say that I have been reelected as her best friend.

"Yup. Want to meet at the usual?" The usual means at the corner, at nine o'clock.

"Okay. And do you want to 'crawl' after shul?" Phyl asks in a muffled giggle.

Hearing her laughter lifts me out of the pit I've been wallowing in all week.

"You really want to crawl again? What if we get caught this time?"

Phyl is silent for a moment. Then, sounding dejected, she asks, "Don't you want to, Mollie?"

"Sure I do. I just don't want to get caught. I'd die of embarrassment. That's all."

The bounce is back in her voice, "Great! See you in the morning. Bye."

Next day during Junior Cong I sit wedged between Naomi and Phyl. It's a safe place, even in my longing and disappointment. But when Naomi turns down our invitation to join us for our post-salami escapade, thoughts of revenge dance in my head until Phyl's zest for adventure sweeps them aside.

When we think everyone has left the building, including Wayne the janitor, and when Phyl and I have checked all the bathrooms to make certain no stragglers remain, we set about crawling. It's our game of mystery, intrigue, espionage, set in our shul. It's a game that's certain to carry me as far away from my current misery as I can go.

Confident that no one is around, we pretend we're assigned a top-secret mission. This involves navigating our way from the doors of the main sanctuary all the way to the platform (the bimah) at the front of the sanctuary where the rabbi, the cantor and various other men lead the congregation in prayer, and where stands the Ark containing the Torah scrolls. Females are not permitted on the bimah in an Orthodox shul.

There are three long aisles leading from the doors at the back to the bimah at the front. There is the middle aisle separating men from women, and an aisle on either side. The trick is to make the journey without being detected by the enemy circling above. To do this, we have to get down on all fours and crawl.

Used to be that the enemy was nobody in particular. Today in my head I've given them a name.

The journey begins. After several heart-stopping moments, we arrive at our destination in one piece. We're handed a map by a friend. The map will guide us to safety. We must go to the rooms next to, and behind, the bimah. Much to our surprise (no matter how many times we see it) there is a tiny room just to the left of the bimah. We enter through a secret passageway that leads from the doors at the back of the bimah (on either side of the Ark).

A band of sunbeams shines through the long narrow window at one end of this tiny room. Dust particles dance in the rays. On the floor-to-ceiling bookcases lie weathered prayer books, boxes of black, white or purple wrinkled satin skullcaps, and a small collection of wine cups, spice boxes, candlesticks and other objects used in religious rituals. We never touch anything — that's the rule.

Just in front of the long window is a winding metal staircase that seems to lead up to nowhere. The steps are so narrow we imagine only fairy feet could climb them. On tiptoe we work our way up the metal spiral, step by step, until at last we reach our destination. The top step opens onto a small balcony that would hold the choir, if we had one. Our hearts leap as we look down upon the assembled masses who have come to hear us thrill them with arias of inexpressible beauty.

Next the map tells us to explore the corridors and rooms behind the stage in the auditorium. Down, down, down the spiral we go, uncoiling like snakes, and then fly out of the main sanctuary and down, down, down we go until we reach the auditorium two floors below. We climb the few steps onto the stage, slip behind the enormous green velvet curtains and finally exit through a door, stage right.

Before us looms a corridor with several doors lining each wall. We scurry up and down the corridor, panting with fear of capture, then we try each doorknob. Most weeks every door is locked.

Phyl turns a doorknob. It springs all the way to the left. She opens it a crack.

"Oh no! The door opened. Oh no! Oh no! What do I do?" Phyl has a half-giddy, half-panicked look about the eyes.

"Calm down, Phyl. Just peek inside." I'm too cowardly myself to step closer.

Obediently she pushes the door open wide, and for a long moment stands gaping inside.

"What is it? What do you see?" I imagine someone's hot breath on my neck.

She has a peculiar look on her face. "It's a swimming pool, or maybe a giant bathtub. It's at the bottom of a long staircase. Everything is tiled, I think. I can't really tell 'cause it's so dark down there."

We can't turn on the lights because it's the Sabbath and it is forbidden to turn electricity on or off, to do any work, during the Sabbath. I edge closer, confident now that there is something monstrous down there.

"Wow!" I exhale in relief. "I've never seen a pool like this before. So many steps leading down to it. But there's no water in it. Do you think this is the ritual bath, the mikvah?"

"Yeah, it must be," Phyl replies. "I wonder why the door wasn't locked today."

"Should we go down to the bottom?" I'm hoping Phyl will nix my suggestion. But she's always ready for an adventure. I follow her, step by step. At last we are at the bottom. Underfoot is what looks like a drain. It is cool down here, and our voices bounce off the white tiles. We've struck gold!

For several minutes we stand around and sit around and sprawl around, wondering about the people who use this ritual bath. We try to imagine them naked. We wonder what they actually do or say when they are here. We wonder why they choose to perform this ritual. In the dim light from the hallway above our heads spin with images of naked bodies.

Then the light changes. A shadow ensnares us. My heart shoots into my throat. Phyl grabs my forearm and squeezes it ferociously.

We look up towards the door at the top of the staircase. The silhouette of a large man stands still. Silent. We stand still. Silent. Please God, don't punish us for being here. We're just kids. We were just exploring. We'll never do anything wrong again if you save us this time, we promise. Please, please.

Blood rushing through my head deafens me. This is the end.

"Who's down there?"

"We are," we reply in unison, voices quivering.

"Who's 'we'? Get up here this minute."

We dash up the long staircase. I bash my left shin against the top step as I trip into the hallway. I stay bent over to rub it and at the same time twist my head up to see who he is.

Peering down at us is Wayne, the janitor. With a half-smile, half-smirk, he scratches his head and says, "What are you crazy girls up to *now*?"

Phyl begins to convulse. For a moment there, she too saw something monstrous towering above her from the top of the stairs. And now she is safe. She is where she belongs.

Her laughter starts small, but it grows. Grows into a roaring laugh. Grows until it fills the corridor, the entire shul, the entire Jewish community, and the entire world of adults' mysterious, secret ways.

29

AFTER PHYL AND I bid one another a fond farewell, I stroll towards home. It's exciting to have a scare now and then, especially when the ending is a happy one.

As I approach my front door, a chorus of voices calls out my name. Standing in a huddle on Kelsey's porch are Kelsey, Betty, Chris, Betty's brother Jim and Chris' brother Kenny. Their cheeks are the colour of autumn apples, their eyes twinkling in the noon sun.

"Want to hang around with us this aft?" Kelsey asks politely.

"Uh ... well ... I don't know. Last time we were all together it didn't go too well."

Chris, being older and all, jumps in, "You're not going to harp on that, are you?"

"Uh ... I guess not."

"Good. Then why don't you get out of those fancy church duds and come back out."

My mother looks moderately surprised when I announce my plan to hang around with the neighbourhood kids for the afternoon. She mumbles something like, "Remember, you can always come home if things get out of hand again. You're not going to change their ideas overnight."

I join the group and Chris suggests we work on a snow sculpture in her backyard. At first everything seems fine. I throw myself into the fun. By mid-afternoon we're frosty. Then Chris whispers something to both Betty and Kelsey which I can't quite catch.

"Sorry, what did you say, Chris?"

"Oh, nothing."

"Oh, I thought you said something to us."

"I said something to Betty and Kelsey."

"Why not to me too?" My face is hot and distorted.

"Because it's not for your ears, okay?"

"Oh.... Well, why not?"

"Because I invited them into my house for some hot chocolate, but I think it would be better if you went home, don't you?"

"Why would it be better?"

"Because we don't serve Jewish food at my house."

"I don't need Jewish food, I don't need any food. I thought we were hanging around together, that's all."

"Yes, well, now we're cold and we want to go in for a while. If we come back out later, maybe we'll let you know."

"Chris," Kelsey interrupts, "why can't Mollie join us?"

"Because my parents really wouldn't appreciate it, that's why."

"Never mind. Don't bother, Kelsey. I know it's not your fault."

At that moment there's a rattling of the back doorknob. There stands Chris' mother, tall and lean with tightly permed hair and sharp arching eyebrows. She surveys the situation.

"Chris, get in here," she orders, lips stretched thin.

Chris obeys.

In a flash she comes back to us. "Me and my brother have to go in now," she says.

The rest of us begin to drift away to our own homes.

"Sorry, Mollie," Kelsey says in a voice even sadder than I feel.

"You're a good friend. Thanks for sticking up for me."

"Want to come to my house for hot chocolate?"

"Oh, that's okay, Kels. Thanks anyway, but I sort of feel like going home now."

"I understand."

A few minutes later, perched upon the couch, I stare out at Chris' house across the street. My face is still burning. I vow never to step foot on her property again. Who wants her hot chocolate anyway? The same goes for monkey-see, monkey-do Betty. Elizabeth Anne said it herself, we're different. There's no getting around it.

Gradually my anger begins to melt; instead I begin to feel ugly. Why did I have to be born different? Why does everything have to be so complicated? And where is Naomi when I need her most?

Just then I notice the front door open at Chris' house. I imagine her coming across the street to beg my forgiveness. Instead, Betty and Jim trudge up her front walk, where they are welcomed into the house by a smiling Kenny and Chris.

"You creeps!!" I scream through the window locked shut against the winter cold.

The moisture from my breath leaves an oval that quickly shrivels on the pane.

"Mollie? Did you call me?"

"I *hate* them, Mom. I hate everybody!"

30

WHEN NAOMI WANDERS by at recess on Monday, Elizabeth Anne and I are working at a conversation.

"Mollie, I hope your feelings weren't hurt by that talk we had last week about ... you know ..."

"Religion?"

"Yes. Maybe honesty isn't the best policy when it comes to friendship and religion."

"Maybe."

"You don't seem like your old self, Moll. Are you mad at me?"

I glance at Naomi, who's eavesdropping. She grins a shy grin. Her eyelids are blinking triple-time.

"I'll be okay, Elizabeth Anne. Don't worry about me."

As we head back into school, Naomi comes up to me.

"Mollie, could we get together next Saturday afternoon after shul?"

I pounce on the offer.

"Of course!"

Oh, joy! She's coming back to me.

Saturday hasn't looked so good in a long time. There's a bounce in my step as I wash and dress for shul, planning the menu of activities for Naomi if we end up at my house in the afternoon. I'm eating breakfast when the doorbell rings. Odd. No one ever rings our doorbell at nine o'clock on a Saturday morning.

"I'll get it," I call out to my mother. My father left the house with my brothers at least fifteen minutes before. "Maybe Dad or the guys forgot something important."

I open the wooden door. I reach for the handle of the screen door, but stop short. No one is there. No person. Just a muddy smudge almost the entire length and width of the glass section of the door. No, not just a smudge. It has a distinct shape. It looks like this 卐 . A swastika. The Nazi symbol.

My arms explode in currents of goosebumps and my ears tingle. Scenes flash by in a split second: they're dragging me and my brothers away from our parents, all is lost. None of this makes sense. This is my safe little neighbourhood, I'm in my house with my mother. How can there be a swastika on our window?

"Mollie, who's at the door?"

"It's ... it's ..."

"Who rang the bell?"

"I ... I don't know! Come here, Mom. Come quick, okay?"

My mother limps to the front door, one shoe on, one shoe half-on. She looks straight ahead and her mouth flies open. It's almost funny.

"Go into the kitchen," she commands in a voice I've never before heard from her. "I'm going outside for a minute."

"No, I'm scared. I want to be with you, Mom." Is this the beginning of the nightmare? I don't want to be alone!

She understands.

"Okay, okay. I just want to check around the outside of the house." What's she checking for? Does she suspect the place is surrounded by enemies hiding in the bushes? If we find whatever it is she's searching for, then what do we do?

Slowly we tour the outside of the house. The basement windows and several main floor windows have been branded. Our house is encrusted with mud, our home violated. But to my great relief, there's no one in sight.

Maybe it's my fault this has happened. Too much talk about religion, too much curiosity about the past ...

"We'll clean these off later," my mother says wearily. "Let's go inside now."

I've lost my appetite for shul, even for being with Naomi. But my mother won't let it go.

"It's important to honour your commitments, Mollie."

I've heard this before.

"Okay, but can I tell Naomi about this ... this thing?"

"Perhaps we should wait until we know who did it. I'll talk it over with Dad on the way home and we'll go from there. We don't want to alarm Naomi and Phyl."

"Phyl is home with a bad cold. It's just Nao. Can I tell her?"

"I wish you wouldn't. She might worry that something will happen to her."

"Mom, she's got other things on her mind."

"There are only so many ways a person can say 'no' and I think I've tried all of them," my mother says with a tiny grin.

"Thanks, Mom."

31

ALL THROUGH Junior Cong I rehearse exactly how I'll describe the event to Naomi. I want her to be shocked enough to be impressed, but not so shocked she'll have nightmares and then I'll be in trouble for spilling the beans. As we're heading downstairs for our salami on rye, I drop a hint of things to come.

"What do you mean 'someone attacked' your house?"

"I'll tell you later. I'm not supposed to tell."

"Were these people actually in your house?"

"Nao, we'll talk about it on the way home; I promise."

This sounds crazy, but I'm almost glad it happened. It gives me something to offer to Naomi, something that might attract her back into my life. I want her to remember how exciting our time together used to be.

On the way home I describe the details. All of them are true, maybe just a bit exaggerated. This is only to make sure that Naomi understands the significance of the event.

"Are you sure it's safe for us to go back to your house?"

"Of course it is! My whole family is there, even my father."

"We could go for a walk instead."

"And miss out on all the things I have planned for us?"

"Well, okay, but I probably shouldn't stay too long."

Usually there's a cosy calm over our house, a Saturday peacefulness. Today there's quiet chaos, as though nothing is in its proper place, but no one is mentioning it out loud.

"I'm going out to wipe the windows," my father says to my mother.

"Be careful," she says.

He comes back in casually, as if he were back from an ordinary chore.

Naomi and I settle in for a few rounds of Chinese checkers in my bedroom. Things are almost normal.

The doorbell rings. We jump out of our skins. Naomi grabs my arm and stares into my face. I stare back.

"I'll get that," my father calls out.

"We'll come with you, Dad," I shout from my room. We scramble up from the floor and head towards the door. My father puts his ear to the wooden panel and listens. Then he opens it.

No one is there. He opens the screen door and walks out onto the front porch. We follow. I'm holding onto the back of his sweater vest, and Naomi is holding onto the back of my dress.

"Dirty Jew! Dirty Jew!" a boy's voice bellows from across the street.

"Who's out there? Who are you?" my father shouts into the daylight as though it were dense fog. We see no one. There is only the voice.

"I know that voice, Dad. That's Kenny, Chris' older brother."

Suddenly Kenny's head appears above the fence surrounding their house. Then we see Jim's head, Betty's brother. And then Chris' and Betty's. This is a game for them. I see the wild expression on their faces. I've seen that expression before. On Naomi's face at the mall, on Phyl's at a shul crawl.

On my own.

"It's just a game, Dad. I don't think they really mean anything by it."

"You damned brats!" my father's voice blasts across the street. He turns to go back inside. Naomi is clutching my arm just above the elbow as though the touch can protect her. Her eyes get that overcast look, that cloudy-with-a-chance-of-rain look.

"You dirty Jews! Kikes! Kikes!" No, not a game. For a fraction of a second my father stands like a statue, stunned. Then, mouth twisted, he snaps at us to come inside. This is no game. I want to stay outside and hurl every wretched, horrid word I know back across to their side. But my father's tone tells me we'd better follow him.

"Will they be back, Dad?"

"No, they'll never do this again. I'll see to it." My father doesn't seem like himself. I want him back to normal, to his quiet background self. This angry man scares me; he seems like someone else's father.

"How come you're so upset, Dad? They're just Betty's and Chris' brothers. It's not like they can hurt us."

"You're right, they can't and won't hurt us! But sometimes smoke turns into fire. We shouldn't be subjected to this treatment by *anyone*."

Naomi's eyelids are going berserk. "I ... I ... uh ... I think I should go home now, in case they attack again."

"Attack? For Pete's sake, Nao, they aren't armed and dangerous. Would you relax please?"

"I can't."

"Why not? We're safe here. My mom and dad are right here."

This seems to make her even more upset.

"I'd like to go now, Mollie. I want to eat dinner at home tonight."

"What's so exciting at home?"

"Nothing. I'm ... I'm helping my mother more. She needs me ..."

"Your mother is so nice. She's gentle, isn't she?"

"Yes." Naomi's entire face transforms into a crying grin — her lips are smiling while her eyes are crying.

"What's wrong, Nao? Did I hurt your feelings?"

"No, no, no! Stop asking me all the time whether you've hurt my feelings!"

Neither of us says anything.

Then Naomi flicks a tear from her cheek, lets out an enormous sigh, and smiles a genuine smile.

"Want a best two out of three Chinese checkers before you leave?"

While we play, Naomi seems to relax. Sunbeams stream into my bedroom and sparkle on the marbles.

Then, without meaning to, I start to laugh.

"What are you laughing about?" Naomi asks defensively.

"Sorry! Sorry, I can't help it. I was just thinking about the time, it was a few years ago, when you and I were listening to the news on the radio. They were talking about guerrilla warfare, and we thought that a bunch of gorillas had come down out of the hills to stir up trouble. Remember?"

"Yeah, and then you asked your mother whether there were any gorillas in Canada? And when we told her why we were asking, she nearly split her side laughing."

"We didn't know then that Kenny and Jim were guerrillas."

"How are you spelling that?"

I jump to my feet and act out the big hairy

kind. For a moment we can both laugh. But I can't wash my eyes of the image of Betty and Chris and Kenny and Jim doubled over with mean-spirited laughter. Their laughter echoes behind mine.

32

I N THE EVENING MY parents speak privately in
their bedroom. As hard as I strain to eavesdrop,
it is impossible to decipher their whisperings. At
last they come out. My mother marches to the
telephone. It soon becomes clear who is on the
other end. It's a relief to know that she's handling
it. It would be too much for me on my own.

"Well, perhaps they didn't learn it in your
home, but they're picking it up somewhere....
Yes, I think an apology is in order.... Okay then.
Goodbye."

My parents dart back to their room to continue
whispering. Finally they call me in.

My father's voice is back to normal.

"You don't have to worry about those kids any
more. Their parents will see to it that they leave
us alone."

"What if they don't?"

"Then you tell us and we'll settle it once and for all."

And I know that they will.

The next afternoon, Sunday, the doorbell rings. I answer. I know that my parents are listening from the livingroom.

Standing there in a clump, eyes cast down, is the gang.

"Sorry," mumbles Chris.

"Sorry," mutter the other three.

"Okay," I say, embarrassed by their embarrassment.

"Would you tell your mother and father 'sorry' too?" Chris asks.

"Sure. Or do you want to tell them yourselves?"

"No, it's okay. You can."

They leave our porch. They'd been my friends, my neighbourhood friends. I don't understand how someone can call you "friend" and share secrets with you, and at the same time hate you. Just because you're different. How can they like me and hurt me, like me and hate me?

I begin to wonder what Chris and the others think a Jew is. Maybe they imagine all sorts of horrid things that aren't true. Maybe they like to scare themselves, the way Naomi and Phyl and I do, but the scary stories are about us. But how could anybody be scared of us? I look at my family, and nothing makes any sense. My head is playing tricks on me. Chris and the others have gotten all jumbled up in my mind with Christ-killers and swastikas. It feels like a barbed wire fence has been installed around our house.

33

HARSH WINTER WINDS are blasting against our windows. The whole house feels jiggly. Our harbour never freezes, but this day it would if it could. The seagulls are hiding somewhere, not bothering to scavenge. I peek out my bedroom window at Kelsey's backyard. Even old Blackie is hibernating. School has been cancelled because of the storm. I love when this happens, especially when it's a Monday. I could do some school work, but I don't feel like it. I decide to take the plunge and call Naomi.

"She's busy," snorts mopey Moe.

"Again?" I sound every bit as annoyed as he does.

"Well, wait a minute." Then he lets out one of those wild yells of his where his tonsils fly out of his mouth. After a longer than normal amount of time, Naomi comes to the phone.

"Hello?"

"Hi, it's me. What are you doing?"

"Just talking with my mother."

"About what?"

"Nothing special."

"Do you want to talk on the phone for awhile?"

"Um, well, my mother's waiting for me to get back to our conversation."

"I thought you said you weren't talking about anything special."

"Mollie, please stop this."

"Stop what?"

"You know what."

"No, I don't know what."

"I told you that I can't tell you why things have changed for me. Maybe some day my parents will let me. But for now I can't explain. I'm sorry. It's not your fault."

"Well, you're making it seem like it's my fault, like I did something to hurt you and now you don't want to be my friend any more."

"I do want to be your friend. If you're my friend, then don't make me tell you things that I'm not supposed to tell."

"What's a friend if you don't talk together, if you don't share your secrets?"

"If you feel that way, then maybe we should cancel our friendship for awhile."

"That's exactly what *you've* been doing — cancelling our friendship. If you want to make it official, then it's okay by me."

"Fine," she says. I can almost hear the fluttering of her eyelashes.

"Fine," I say. And that is that.

The next day at school she looks the other way when she sees me coming. So then I look the other way. It doesn't take much to rip apart the threads of a friendship once you set your heart on it.

For the next several weeks we avoid contact except when absolutely necessary, like at Hebe or during lunch at school or when we have to cook together in Home Ec. During these times we speak in odd little snippets with tight lips. Sometimes it all seems so funny that I want to laugh, but I don't notice any such signs from Naomi. Phyl and all the others tiptoe around us as though we are seriously ill. It's peculiar just how upset bystanders get when a nearby friendship no longer rubs up against them like an affectionate cat.

34

FEBRUARY PASSES. The first week of March my mother takes me aside for a mother-daughter chat. She tells me that in order to have a friend, one must be a friend. She tells me that Naomi needs me to be her friend. She tells me to phone Naomi and to call a truce. How can I refuse? After all, when your mother *commands*, you must obey. Besides, I've missed Naomi so much. Now I can call and if it doesn't work out, I can tell Naomi it was my *mother's* brilliant idea.

I decide to ask Naomi whether I can come over after school on Friday. Not since last autumn have I seen her parents, except for the occasional time when her father shows up at shul.

"Would that be okay with you, Nao?"

"I'll have to check. Hold the line a minute please."

My ears strain to catch the conversation at the other end, but it's too muffled. When Naomi comes back to the phone, I jump as if I've been caught in the act.

"My mother says it's okay."

"Good! Uh ... you don't sound too enthusiastic."

"No, it's okay. I have to hang up now, Mollie."

In a certain sense I have missed not only Naomi, but her mother too. I've missed her mother in the way you miss Edna the cashier at Buywell's when, after two years of shopping there for your favourite slab of toffee, you finally get to chatting with her and you learn that she has two grandchildren and a whole history, and every time after that when she's ringing up your purchases the two of you chitchat, and then one day shortly after the blossoming of this new relationship you discover that Edna has moved on to another department store chain. There's not a huge gap in your life, but the next time you buy your toffee you feel just a little lost, just a little less part of the Buywell family.

That's the way I missed Naomi's mother. I had just been getting to know that she has a life separate and apart from being Naomi's mother when Naomi snatched herself away from me.

Her mother wears her hair in two thick black braids that she pins around the base of her head and clips into position directly behind her ears. She rarely speaks, and when she does it's with a wispy voice that rattles as it passes over her dry lips.

As Naomi and I climb the steps to her second floor flat, I begin to doubt the wisdom of my suggestion. The house feels strange, abandoned. We go into the kitchen. I look towards the sink where her mother is always standing, washing, peeling, scrubbing.

"She's in her room," Naomi responds to my glance. "I'll be right back."

The kitchen clock gobbles up the minutes. Finally Naomi comes back.

"My mother's busy in the bedroom. Maybe she'll be out later. Want a snack?"

The situation is unhinging my nerves. We eat a few dry crackers, pick the crumbs off the orange-and-brown oilcloth with freshly licked fingertips, and settle in for a best two out of three checkers competition. The clock ticks softly. No mother.

No father. No brother. I wish I'd gone home after school.

"Goodbye," I say. "Thanks. See you tomorrow at shul. Should Phyl and I pick you up?"

"Okay. Goodbye," Naomi answers. Her eyelids are completely out of control.

That night, sleep does not come easily. I peek out through my bedroom curtains. The moon is frozen in the sky. I imagine I hear shrieks poured into the night air.

35

THE NEXT MORNING I'm hoping for the comfort of rituals, wanting the same old routines. But when Phyl and I knock on Naomi's door, there is no answer. Cool shivers run through me. The shrieks from the night before come flooding back. Could they have been real?

"Strange there's no answer," I say to Phyl.

"Yup. I guess they all slept in today."

"Guess so."

I convince Phyl to come with me after shul to walk by Naomi's house again to case the joint. In a way we feel like junior detectives, and in another way there's a queer sensation that crawls over my skin.

The house looks drowsy in the noonday sun. I can't take my eyes off the venetian blinds, still shut like eyelids. What are they hiding in there?

We knock on the door. Naomi opens it. Her hair is helter-skelter, her lips almost blue.

"My mother's dead," she reports flatly.

"Oh," we say.

"She had a weak heart. She's been really sick since before Christmas vacation."

"Oh," we say.

"I won't be at school next week. We have to sit shiva — we're in mourning for a week."

"Okay," we say.

"Bye."

"Bye," we say.

We rush along the sidewalk, not exchanging so much as a sigh. How can a person be here one day and not the next? How can a mother not be here any more? How will Naomi go on living?

At my corner, Phyl leaves me. I fly into the house and call out for my mother. I don't know whether she's home from shul.

"MOM! MOM!"

"Yes, dear. I'm in my bedroom."

There she is, sitting on the bed playing with Ray. He beams a welcome. My mother holds out her arms for me.

"I know, darling, I know."

I fling my arms around my mother's neck and cling for dear life.

36

MARCH MELTS. April brings days that start off with a long-sleeved sweater and peak after school with a T-shirt and pedal pushers. The fragrance of dog droppings is in the air. In the spring, Sunday skating is replaced by family strolls or a drive along the seashore for an ice cream cone.

Ever since her mother died, Naomi has lost her taste for life. There are no more titters, no more fingertips pressed against open lips in amazement over some tidbit or other. Moe's anger is perpetual. Their father has hired a housekeeper, Alice, to clean and cook and iron Naomi's blouses, but there's a layer of dust over the furniture, over the family. Alice's pinched face reminds you of a bad smell.

Naomi's father insists that she come home directly after school on Fridays to help Alice prepare dinner. No more plaza for us. Her father insists that she and Moe accompany him home after shul on Saturdays. Sundays, too, belong to her father. Nightly phone conversations are limited to only a few minutes, making it barely worthwhile dialing. Nothing feels right any more. It's not fair.

One day on our way to Hebe, I finally decide to tackle the topic with Nao.

"Ever since your mother ... uh ... um ... died last month, we haven't actually talked about it."

"Well, I've been busy, Mollie."

"I know, but we used to talk about everything. How can we keep this secret?"

"Well, now you know why I wasn't much fun all this time."

"Why wouldn't you talk about it? Did your parents make you promise?"

"They said that some things in life you don't speak of."

"But why this?"

"Dying is private."

"Oh. I didn't know that."

"Neither did I."

"Do you want to be friends again, Nao?"

"Of course. I always have."

Two tears are rolling down her soft fat cheeks. It hurts to see how sad she is. "My father is acting so weird. I never really knew him before. I guess I only really knew my mom."

"Yeah, I know what you mean."

"My father is so silent. He always has been, but it didn't used to matter. I had my mom to talk to. But now he's all I've got."

"Can you ask him to talk more?"

"I can try."

"You can always tell things to me, Nao. And you can talk to my mom if you like. She's great for that sort of thing. She understands."

"Thanks. Maybe, if I really need to."

Naomi falls into a trance and stares straight ahead for the longest time. Then she says out loud, but more to herself than to me, "Do you still care about me, Mollie?"

"Care about you?? Are you kidding? I love you."

It seems strange to say those words aloud as we casually stroll along to Hebe. They're words that I think but I don't often say. I guess there's more thinking than speaking when it comes to love and death.

37

THE LAST WEEK of May it's Naomi's birthday. Every year she has a birthday party and invites all the girls in the class. It used to be pretty wild with about fifteen girls buzzing around. Her mother always looked at us in amazement, quietly drinking in the chaos, occasionally stroking Naomi's black hair as she passed by.

This year her father and Alice organize a small gathering. Phyl and I arrive together. It's our first time at Naomi's place since her mother died, and a haunting feeling comes over me as we climb the steps to her door.

"Phyl, do you believe in ghosts?"

"Um ... I think so, but I'm not sure. Do you?"

"Well, I don't believe in the kind in white sheets. But I guess there can be sort of a presence, like the dead person is somewhere nearby watching."

"You mean, Naomi's mother is watching us?"

"In a way. I feel she's here, in this house, watching over everyone."

"You're spooking me, Mollie. Stop it."

"Sorry. I didn't mean to spook you. It's just a feeling I have, that's all."

The flat itself seems forlorn, abandoned. The family too appears forsaken, messy, rundown. Not even sweet-smelling cupcakes with pink icing dappled with tiny crunchy silver balls can clear the musty smell.

All eight guests arrive, but the place still feels sad. I want to get away. I give Phyl the "let's get out of here" nod. We excuse ourselves and race off to the bathroom.

"What are you up to, Mollie? I can tell you're planning something."

"I was thinking about the ghost idea. Do you want to look for Nao's mother?" Then my conscience prickles. "We probably shouldn't. It's not very nice. And if we get caught ..."

"Oh come on. We won't get caught. Naomi will never know." It's the same voice Phyl uses for shul crawling.

"Okay, but we might have to explore the whole

flat." A shiver of excitement blots out any other feelings.

The guests are playing parlour games and their laughter shields them from our exploration noises.

"Let's check her clothes closet first. Maybe some of her clothes are still there."

Phyl gives me that wide-eyed frenzied look of hers and begins to whisper, "Uh, you mean, look right into that wardrobe in the corner? Open it and just start looking in there?"

"Of course. How else are we going to find her if we don't search everywhere?"

The wardrobe door squeaks open at the slightest touch, and something inside stirs. It's either Naomi's mother's ghost or a draft of air caught up by opening the door. We're not sure which.

We stand stock still.

"We're dead, Moll. She's in there."

"Let's get out of here!" I grab Phyl by the wrist and race back to the bathroom. We slam the door and lock it from the inside. In an explosion of relief, we begin to cackle. We feel out of control, crazy. We bend over with aching sides, struggling to catch our breath.

A powerful banging on the door sobers us.

"Oh no, someone knows what we're doing! I can tell from the knock. They sound mad," Phyl pants.

"You can't tell from a knock! Sh ... sh! Maybe they'll go away if we're quiet."

Again, powerful banging.

Through the door comes Alice's tight voice, "You girls should be ashamed! Acting like ninnies! Now get yourselves into the kitchen this minute."

The harshness of her adult anger stings us. A trickle of giggles dribbles out of Phyl like the last drips of water from a closed tap. We feel slapped in the face and we know we deserve it.

"Let's go," I say to Phyl, "Nao must be furious we've missed part of her party."

"Well, it wasn't our fault. We were just fooling around. We weren't doing anything wrong."

"No, but still ..."

Naomi approaches us as we head towards the kitchen.

Through clenched teeth she says, "I don't know exactly what you've been doing here today, but I do know you were in my parents' bedroom, giggling your heads off. My mother is dead. I don't find that too funny. Just because you're afraid of something you don't know about doesn't give you the right to make fun of it."

I don't know where to look. I can't stand being myself. I can't believe what I've done. I wish I could exchange places with Naomi's mother. When you've hurt someone you love like I love Nao, you almost wish you weren't around to feel anything.

"Sorry, Nao. Honest. Phyl and I were just being silly. I didn't mean anything by it." I wish I could blame it all on Phyl. I wish I could take it all back.

"That's right. When Mollie got me thinking about ghosts, I got sort of spooked." Phyl wants to punish me for planting the seed in her mind.

Naomi walks away from us. She leaves us to stew in our own juices.

That night I curl up into as tiny a ball as my body will allow. For some reason, images of Chris and Betty crowd my thoughts. They've been mean to me. When we were little kids together, there were the usual shouting matches among us, the usual squabbling, but I wouldn't call it meanness. When you grow up, things change, they get more serious. Back then none of us knew about religion, our own or anyone else's. Now we're divided into separate camps according to our religions. And it's as though their meanness comes out of being afraid. The very idea of a Jew makes them afraid. Their heads are filled with false ideas, frightening ones, ones that scare them.

Phyl and I were definitely mean to Naomi. How could we have been so mean? The hurt is so deep. Maybe we're afraid too. After all, what do we know about death? The thought of a dead mother is frightening, it scares us. No one ever talks about death. It never happens here, it happens to someone else, someone old.

There's no excuse for me, though. I look at the clock on the night table. It's midnight. Things will never be the same again between me and Naomi. I'll never trust Chris and Betty again, no matter what. So why should Naomi ever relax her guard with me? I've dug right into her mother's grave and jostled her bones. Probably her mother will never forgive me either, because I've hurt her child. Things will never be the same.

38

DURING THE NEXT several days at school Naomi turns away from me each time I come near her. I have betrayed her. After that her father carts her off for "a long weekend" in Montreal with her aunt. What her father calls a long weekend is actually a full week.

Maybe, I bargain with myself, by the time she gets back her big heart will have allowed me in. Everything I did will have been erased. I am desperate to speak with her, to make it up to her.

On the afternoon she's to leave, a Friday afternoon, I decide to walk by her house. Even being on her block helps me feel closer to her. As I round her corner, I spot her standing beside her father's car. It's a big old Buick, turquoise with a cream roof. Her father is taking her to the airport. Moe doesn't seem to be going on this trip. He waves goodbye from the porch and then disappears inside. Naomi is pale, miserable, weepy. She's wearing a new plaid jumper that looks too big. Inside the big Buick, she looks like a little kid. I rush to reach her car before she crawls in, but I'm one second too late.

"Nao! Nao!" I call out, but she seems not to hear even though all the windows are open wide. She seems so small and all alone.

"Have a good trip," I say.

She stares back at me, stony. She stares, but will not smile.

As her car turns the corner, a plan takes shape in my mind. I will give Naomi the time she needs for her heart to heal while she's away. Then when she returns I'll shower her with friendship and devotion. Her head will spin. Her heart will leap. My mother will semi-adopt her and we will be stepsisters. I can barely wait for the time to pass.

39

THE FRIDAY AFTERNOON of her return, I decide to buy a gift for her, a peace offering. There's a drugstore around the corner from home with a cosmetics counter at the back. Perhaps something small and pretty would do the trick, "a little something," as my mother always says. Before going up to the cosmetics counter, I circle the inside of the store a few times. I'm not used to making purchases (other than toffee), at least not without Naomi or my mother. There's a special aura that surrounds the cosmetics counter, something dangerous, or romantic.

The woman behind the counter is new. Her hair is so bright, so orange, that I stop in my tracks for a moment and just stare. Not even gale-force winds could stir it. It's sprayed stiff. Her eyebrows have been plucked and in their place she has pencilled in sharp, arching orange lines that veer off towards the tips of her ears. The pancake makeup on her nose spotlights her pores, and on her cheeks it glows like little red bulbs. She is dressed in a duster, bright orange too, that covers her clothes. Pinned on the left lapel is her name tag, which reads "Florence."

She is dusting the glass display cases, and suddenly notices me.

"Hello, dear. May I help you?"

Her voice is softer and smarter than I'd imagined.

"Um, well, I was looking for a present for a friend of mine."

"How nice. How old is your friend?"

"She's my age."

"I see." She pushes her thick orange lips out in front and taps her index finger against them. She is thinking. I am silent, mesmerized. I would gladly spend the rest of my life soaking up her fragrance, her mannerisms, her voice.

"Toilet water is always a welcomed gift," she comments as she bends over to remove a small bottle from the display case.

"Do you think your friend would like toilet water?"

Her orange eyebrows meet in the middle.

"What's wrong, dear? Are you ill?"

I'm speechless, dazed. Then I mumble, "No."

"If there's something else you'd like to take a look at, just say so. That's why I'm here, to help you out."

"That's okay," I answer. "I think I've changed my mind."

She shrugs, smiles weakly, and sets about dusting again.

My cheeks are burning as I make a beeline for the door. All the way home, I compose a letter in my mind's eye. It will be sent to the top manager of the drugstore, and in it will be a full account of the shameful event, the cruel joke, that has just occurred. I will seek justice.

40

NAOMI IS EXPECTED back at six o'clock. I have no present, but at five thirty I park myself under a tree at her corner anyway and wait for her father's car to appear. It doesn't come. At five forty-five her front door opens and out walks her father. He stands on the porch, just staring into space. From time to time he swats away a fly. I begin to imagine that Naomi has been locked away in her flat all week, just pretending to be in Montreal.

Another minute passes and then a taxicab pulls up in front of her house. Naomi climbs out, burdened by her suitcase, and dumps it with a thud onto the pavement. Her father is waiting for her, and I hope she'll notice him immediately so that she won't feel abandoned, not even for a minute.

Her eyelids are fluttering wildly. She spots her

father, who stands rooted like a tree. If her mother were here, she would have rushed up to Naomi and embraced her and examined her for any damage she might have suffered while away from home. But her father just stands waiting for his daughter to come to him, and when she does, he kisses the top of her head and she rests her cheek against his chest and they both cry.

"Nao!" I call out to her. She turns. Then she says something to her father who steps inside the house. This time *she* stands like a tree while I walk quickly towards her.

"Nao, hi!"

"Hi Mollie."

"How was your trip?"

"Very pleasant, thanks."

"Want to get together tomorrow?"

"I don't think I can. I have to pack."

"You mean unpack."

"No, I mean pack. My dad has decided as soon as school ends next week we're moving to Montreal. We want to be in the same city as my aunt."

"You can't be serious."

"Um ... sorry Mollie."

"But ... well ... I mean you don't seem upset at all and I ... well ... I ..." I burst into tears and blubber into a wad of tissues which Naomi hands to me. Good old Naomi. She's always prepared. It makes me cry harder. How will I get by without her?

"We'll be back for visits every year to see my mom's grave."

I think about what Naomi has lost, and what I'm losing seems smaller.

"Are you moving because Phyl and I hurt your feelings so badly?"

"Of course not, silly. We're moving because our dad says we have to. I'd rather stay right here, close to where my mom is. And you."

I can't believe she's forgiving me.

"Do you really mean that, Nao?"

"Yes."

Mostly, I believe her.

41

T HE NEXT DAY at noon I arrive at Naomi's door. The flat is littered with boxes half-packed. The rooms look half-naked.

Things can change so quickly. One minute everything is in its place and the next minute it's topsy-turvy. One minute Naomi's mother is here, loving her with all her heart and the next minute it stops beating. One minute I think that Nao and I will always share our secrets and the next minute we're torn apart. Nothing seems to stay the same.

"How was shul?" she asks.

"I didn't go today. I'm too upset."

We sit on the bed cross-legged. I hand over a tiny paper bag to Naomi.

"Here's a little something," I say, not knowing what to say.

"Thanks very much."

Naomi slowly opens the bag and peeks inside.

"Oh, what pretty wrapping paper. I'm sorry to wreck it."

She crumples the purple tissue paper into a ball and then examines the bottle from all directions.

"It's such a dainty bottle."

"I'm glad you like it," I say almost shyly. "I nearly didn't buy it for you, but my mom explained it to me last night."

"Explained what?"

"Toilet water!"

"You mean *eau de toilette*?"

"Yup."

"Mollie, are you trying to tell me you thought this meant water from a toilet?"

Now she smiles. Then she begins to giggle one of those contagious giggles and keels right over onto her bed and roars and roars and roars. I keel over too and cry and laugh and laugh and cry. I want to stay right here forever with my best friend, with Nao.

After many minutes have passed, I jump up from her bed.

"How about one last reading?" I ask.

"Okay. Rossetti?"

"Yup."

Her poetry book is wending its way to her new home in a moving van, so we do it from memory.

We clear our throats.

For there is no friend like a sister
In calm or stormy weather;
To cheer one on the tedious way,
To fetch one if one goes astray,
To lift one if one totters down,
To strengthen whilst one stands.

"Will you write to me, Nao?"

"Of course!!"

"Me too."

When I leave her bedroom I leave so much behind. I think we'll write. At least, I'm pretty sure we will.